OPIATE JANE

Jessica K. Baker

KiCam
PROJECTS

LIBRARY OF CONGRESS CATALOGING-IN-PUBLICATION DATA
Names: Baker, Jessica K., author.
Title: Opiate Jane / Jessica K. Baker.
Description: Georgetown, Ohio : KiCam Projects, [2019] | Summary: Fifteen-year-old Jane slowly becomes hopeful after she and her little sister are reunited with their mother, until she learns that Landon, her new boyfriend, abuses drugs, like her mother.
Identifiers: LCCN 2019017994 (print) | LCCN 2019021190 (ebook) | ISBN 9781733546256 (ebook) | ISBN 9781733546249 (pbk) | ISBN 9781733546256 (eBook)
Subjects: | CYAC: Drug abuse—Fiction. | Mothers and daughters—Fiction. | Dating (Social customs)—Fiction. | Sisters—Fiction. | Foster children—Fiction.
Classification: LCC PZ7.1.B3515 (ebook) | LCC PZ7.1.B3515 Opi 2019 (print) |
   DDC [Fic]--dc23
LC record available at https://lccn.loc.gov/2019017994

Cover and book design by Mark Sullivan
ISBN 978-1-7335462-4-9 (paperback)
ISBN 978-1-7335462-5-6 (ebook)

Printed in the United States of America

Published by KiCam Projects
Georgetown, Ohio

www.KiCamProjects.com

Dedication

For everyone who needs a second chance

Table of Contents

- Third time's a charm ... 1
- Off to farm school ... 14
- Tornado warning and the witch ... 24
- Freaky lunch friends ... 35
- Paintball wars ... 44
- Great! It's party time ... 57
- More stormy weather ... 63
- Confessions ... 72
- Missing ... 82
- Lessons ... 92
- Little green monsters ... 97
- The truth hurts ... 104
- Shut down ... 119
- What was I thinking? ... 130
- Stowaway ... 138
- Enough ... 150
- Acknowledgments ... 165

Some will tell us there is no such thing as Monsters.

They are wrong.

There is a Monster in our world.

It lives in disguise.

It hides beneath the faces of our family, our friends, and our loved ones.

Taking them over and replacing them with someone unknown.

The Monster is Addiction.

How do I make the Monster go away?

Third time's a charm

She was going to do it again. I knew she was. We'd been through this twice before. How could the judge even have considered placing us back in her care? Judges aren't as smart as they think they are. Last time, we were with her for seven months before they came for us. It took them six months to check on us, and by that time, we'd been alone three-quarters of the time. It had only taken her a month to go back to her old ways. Evidently a Friday-through-Sunday weekend wasn't long enough for Mother. She needed to spend most of her week out getting high too. I honestly don't know how she could afford to do it like that. But this time, she'd spent thirty days in some rehab and had gotten a cleaning job at some big house in no-man's land, where we were supposed to live in the garage apartment. Mother had said the house was really old, so I figured we'd be staying in the servants' quarters. And of course, it was in a different school district, so I'd be starting a new school in March of my sophomore year. Great! Why couldn't they just let me finish my school year where I was? It would be the third one this year. This was a waste of time. They'd come back for us. They always did.

So there we were in the car driving an hour away from St. Bernard, where I'd lived for the past three months. I had always lived in Cincinnati; St. Bernard is a suburb. City life was what I knew. Mother always liked to stay in the Over-the-Rhine area. It was more convenient for her that way. Now we were headed to some town called Winchester. What, did they make guns there?

I'd never heard of it and I didn't want to go. One of the other foster kids had told me it was in some really poor county that didn't have anything and was full of farmers and hillbillies. She sure didn't sugar-coat it.

We were about forty minutes into the drive before my mother said a word to me. She and Lizzie had been chatting in the front seat. Mother wasn't responsible enough to realize Lizzie was too small to be sitting up there. Ohio had child-restraint laws and Lizzie should have been in the back of the car. She was only four years old and wasn't big enough to be out of a booster seat, let alone in the front of the car. I knew I should have said something, but I really didn't want to sit up there with Mother. Lizzie was so excited to see her mommy and to be going home. She was even more ecstatic when I offered her the front seat. I think she honestly thought I was doing her some kind of favor. The poor kid, she was just too young to realize what kind of person Mother really was. I guess I'd made sure she didn't know what kind of mother she had. I'd spent the last year of foster care lying to Lizzie and telling her how much Mother loved her even though they weren't together. I told her all the good stories about Mother before she'd started using the drugs. Now Lizzie barely knew her but thought she'd hung the moon. I knew I shouldn't have done that, but the kid needed something to look forward to, and hearing stories about her wonderful mother really made her day.

I looked up to see Mother watching me in the rearview mirror. I would have to say she did look better. She must have gained about twenty pounds and she'd cleaned herself up with a new haircut and makeup. She gave me a look that was riddled with guilt and then asked me why I'd been so quiet. She might have felt guilty, but I knew it wouldn't stop her from going back to her true love. The remorse wouldn't last long, and Lizzie and I would be the mess she'd leave behind again. I wasn't about to make small talk with her. I gave her a "hmph" and returned to staring out the window.

We finally came to another stoplight; I think it had been about ten minutes since the last one. We turned left into a little town. To the right were a small, older motel and a Subway. It was a strange-looking Subway that seemed more like it should have been a house than a restaurant. There was a white house that looked completely out of place in front of the motel. I saw a gas station, some other building, and a car wash. Houses lined both sides of the street. It took us about a minute to get to a stop sign. There was a hair salon on one corner and an abandoned gas station on the other. The sign at the gas station said gas was $1.03 a gallon, so clearly it had been empty for a while. We turned left at the stop sign, so I didn't get to see any more of Main Street. Once we made our left, it was houses again, a church, some railroad tracks, and some kind of weird-looking corn-shucking building. I don't know what it was; it had some weird, round buildings and a big barn-looking thing. I figured corn shucking was what they did around there. Hell, it could have been that Winchester shotgun factory for all I knew.

Everything was so drab. The grass was really brown, but it was only the beginning of March, so I started hoping it would green up soon. It just had to or I didn't think I would survive in this town. Granted, the grass can be brown and the trees bare in the city too, but you don't notice it as much with all the asphalt around. Out in the country, all you saw was the brown. It was depressing. I would rather look at asphalt and tall buildings all day than that.

We made a right onto Crum Road. I thanked God it was paved and then I prayed to God to keep us on a paved road. If we were to turn onto anything that resembled a dirt road, I was going to start to think we had entered into the movie *Wrong Turn*. And sure enough, just as the thought rolled through my head, we turned onto gravel. Since technically it wasn't a dirt road, I thought maybe I would be okay. The road was named Melblanc Road. *What a strange name*, I thought.

We turned onto a lane I guessed was a driveway. There was a mailbox at the end, so it had to be a driveway, right? Then I saw it. It was a monstrosity of a house. It was a wonder I hadn't seen it from the highway. It was white and huge, kind of like one of those old plantation houses but much bigger. Oh, yay! I was pretty sure the plantation houses were the ones that had the servants' quarters. I *so* guessed that one right. The house was three stories high, with one part going up to a fourth floor with a rounded roof. It almost looked like something Rapunzel's hair should have been hanging out of. There were huge oak trees and numerous smaller trees in front of the house. That house had to be hundreds of years old. It had a very old style to it but looked as if it were brand new. The house was so white it gleamed from the sunshine that was finally poking through the clouds. The porch was immaculate. There were four high-back rocking chairs slowly rocking from the light March winds that were still blowing after the rain had passed through. It was a little eerie to see those chairs rocking as if someone were sitting in them. The house looked old enough to be haunted. Around the corner of the house was a four-car garage, and to the side of that was a small building with a little porch on the front of it. How odd; that building looked totally out of place there. Then my mother pulled our 1999 Honda Accord up next to it and I knew this was our new so-called home.

Lizzie was shouting, "Let me see my room, Mommy! Let me see my room!" Mother had been telling her all about it during our drive. Mother had been living there for three months already. She had to have a home and a job for three months before she was eligible to get us back after she came out of rehab. I was pretty sure they'd probably given her some random drug screens during that time too. At least I hoped so.

Aunt Darlene had gotten her the job with the Whitmans. Evidently they were one of the richest families in the area. Aunt Darlene went to church with them, and I think we were a charity experiment: *See what happens if you take a family out of the gutter and place them with good people. That's all they need, right? That will fix them.* Aunt Darlene and my mother didn't get along at all, but my aunt had declared herself a good Christian woman and had decided to help my mother out.

A woman who was maybe in her early forties came out from the back door of the monstrous house. She was tall and thin. She had blonde hair that was feathered into some kind of eighties hairstyle. She was dressed in a plaid pin skirt and a very expensive-looking button-up blouse. She wore four-inch heels even though she was already very tall. She was wearing way too much makeup. I had to wonder how she washed off all that black gunk from her eyes every day.

She walked toward my mother and called, "Clara, these must be your girls! I'm so glad they'll finally be joining us."

She looked directly at me and the ring in my nose and asked, "How was your ride, dear?"

The question was sincere, but the look on her face was one of disgust. If I'd been a mind reader, I would have said she was probably wondering what she had gotten herself into.

My mother looked at me and said, "Jane, this is Mrs. Whitman. She's been kind enough to let us use her guest house while I work here."

When I looked at Mrs. Whitman, I caught her staring at the worn-out Chucks on my feet. I acknowledged her anyway. Hell, I even threw in a compliment.

"It's nice to meet you," I said. "You have a really nice house."

Lizzie came running around the car to Mrs. Whitman, started tugging on the woman's shirt, and shouted, "Can I see my room, lady?"

Mrs. Whitman stifled a laugh and told her she could. She excused herself and then headed back into her huge house.

We started unloading the trunk of the car and carrying our things into our little house. We walked through the front door into a kitchen/living room combination. It was small but very nice. There was an archway at the other side of the living room that led into a small hallway. There was a bathroom straight ahead of the hallway, a bedroom to the left, and a bedroom to the right. Lizzie and I were to share a bedroom. Lizzie wasn't too happy about that, but I didn't mind. The last foster home we were in, we'd shared a room with two other girls, so I figured we could survive this situation. The bedroom had two twin beds. I was sure Children Services probably made that some kind of stipulation of Mother getting us back. Last time we lived with her, we'd been lucky to have a mattress on the floor. We'd started off with beds, but it hadn't taken Mother long to get hard up for cash and sell them. She'd sold everything we had. She'd even sold the iPod that St. Vincent de Paul had gotten me for Christmas that year. It hadn't mattered to her that it was the only thing I had besides my clothes. She'd needed a fix and it was worth a quick twenty bucks. She told me I'd lost it, but I found the pawn shop receipt that showed she'd sold it.

Mother came into the room and asked us how we liked it. Lizzie ran up to Mother, hugged her, and shouted, "I love it, Mommy! I do, I do!"

Lizzie was always shouting. She was such a happy little girl for someone who had been through so much in her short life.

Mother was glaring at me, so I knew it was my turn to answer her question.

"It will do," I said. "I'm not unpacking my crap, though. I'm pretty sure we won't be here long. Lizzie can put her stuff anywhere she wants; I'll only be sleeping in here anyway."

I dropped my two backpacks on the bed by the window and sat down next to them.

We were lucky that what few belongings we had were in backpacks. Last time we'd changed foster homes, our stuff had been in brown paper bags. Jennifer, our last foster mom, bought the backpacks for us before we left. She said it was bad enough that we had so little, the least she could do was give us something decent to put it in.

Jennifer was a nice woman; her husband worked as a truck driver and wasn't home much. Jennifer had kept us fed and clean. She hadn't taken too much interest in us, though. She was too busy lingering on the internet all the time. I'm pretty sure she was addicted to Facebook, but she was nice to us. That's a lot for a foster parent. Trust me: They can get bad.

The first time we were taken from Mother, they'd split us up. Lizzie was a baby, four months old. We were separated for eight months. I worried about her so much. I had taken care of her from the day she'd come home from the hospital. When we were placed back with Mother the first time, Lizzie didn't even know who I was. She'd just turned one and was walking. I had missed her so much. I will never know if the home she'd been placed in had taken good care of her. I hated that I didn't know anything about those months of her life. Thank goodness she was too young to remember it!

I'd been placed in a home I referred to as the Daniels Dungeon. The Danielses had remodeled their basement into three bedrooms, which meant they could house nine to twelve kids. They were totally into foster care for a check. The remodel consisted of slapping paneling on the moldy walls and putting carpet right on top of the concrete floor. Every time it rained, the carpet would get soaked under my bed. I spent my entire stay there with a runny nose and a sore throat. I know there had to be a ton of mold under that carpet. But the wet carpet was nothing compared to the smell coming from the four cats that stayed upstairs. We weren't allowed to spend much time up there, but the smell made its way downstairs. We had to go to our rooms right after school and stay there until supper. We ate supper, did multiple chores, and returned to our rooms. They had a bathroom down in the Dungeon. We weren't even allowed to enter the one upstairs. Mr. and Mrs. Daniels must have been miserable, because they would start arguing as soon as he got home from work and would not stop until about one or two in the morning. It never escalated to the point the police needed to be called, but I think that was only because the neighboring house was empty.

"Jane, what do you two want for lunch?" Mother asked.

Coming out of my memory of the Danielses and their dungeon, I thought, *Wow! She's going to cook for us. Wonder how long that will last.*

"You can fix whatever you want; I'm not hungry. I lost my appetite this morning in the courtroom," I answered sarcastically.

"I want pancakes!" yelled Lizzie.

"Okay, little one, pancakes it will be," Mother told her.

I followed them out of the bedroom to the kitchen, then went out the front door to the car to get the rest of Lizzie's stuff, not that she had much. Just as I loaded up my arms, I heard the sound of an engine roaring to life and about dropped everything I was holding. I'd forgotten we were right next to a four-car garage. I went inside to the bedroom to put Lizzie's belongings away. Again, I heard the sound of an engine. I glanced out the window to see a brand-new Ford Mustang pulling out of the garage. The tinted windows were rolled down so I could see the teenage boy driving it. I could tell by the flashy car, the dark sunglasses, and the way he shook his head when he turned toward Mother's car that he was an arrogant ass. *Great, I hope he goes to some expensive private school,* I thought. I sure didn't want to go to a school where everyone knew my mother was his maid. I guess that wouldn't have been as bad as them knowing she was a heroin addict. Then again, depending on the school, the maid thing could have been worse.

Mother would say she was a "recovering" heroin addict. I didn't believe that. She'd been clean before and had gone right back to it. She hadn't always been an addict. When I was little, she'd worked hard to make sure I was cared for. It had always been just me and her. I didn't know anything about my father and I was forbidden to ask. I'd never really thought that much about it. Mother and I had been happy. She went to work and I went to the babysitter. She came home and we would go to the park, take a walk, go on a picnic, or just hang out at home. She met Lizzie's father, Cole, when I was eight. He was okay. He took up more of her time than I'd liked, but she seemed happy. By the time I turned nine, he had moved in. Three months after he moved in, Mother's knee was crushed in a car accident and she was prescribed Vicodin. Her addiction started innocently. She was in pain, so she took her medication. Then she started taking more and more of her medication. Her cast was off and she was still complaining of pain and taking her medication. I realized there was a problem when I couldn't get her to wake up in the middle of the day. That had struck me as odd since she'd been an active person and had never taken naps. I hadn't thought much of it at the time. I was only nine years old and I didn't know anything about drugs. I didn't know that if someone was sitting up and nodding off so badly that they dropped their cigarette, or that if they constantly had funny-looking white snot coming out of their nose, they might be doing drugs.

When I was eleven, Mother found out she was pregnant. By that time, Cole had been gone for a few months. He'd grown tired of Mother's drug use and had taken off to his brother's place in Florida. It was a shame Lizzie never got to meet him. He wasn't that bad of a guy. Mother never told him she was pregnant, and she refused to tell our social worker who Lizzie's father was. I think she knew that if she did, they would have let Cole have Lizzie and she would never have stood a chance of getting her back. When Lizzie was three, Mother heard that Cole had been killed in a freak accident working for a pipeline in Illinois. Lizzie would never know him at all. Mother was sure to let Children Services know his name then, because she wanted to get Social Security benefits for Lizzie. That was so typical of her—more money meant more drugs. I guess Mother hadn't thought that one through, because the state ended up being the one to collect Lizzie's check. Mother couldn't collect it since she didn't have custody of Lizzie. Not long after that, she started working on getting clean.

I'm not sure when she started using heroin. She might have been using it while she was pregnant with Lizzie. That would have explained Lizzie's colic. Lizzie cried the first three months of her life. I know because I took care of her. I found a needle in Mother's bedside table when Lizzie was about two months old. The overdose happened when Lizzie was four months old. That is how Children Services had gotten involved with our family.

I found Mother unconscious on the kitchen floor while Lizzie wailed from the bedroom. I'd been at school all day so I had no idea how long Lizzie had been alone and crying or how long Mother had been unconscious. I tried to wake Mother up, but it was no use; she was not responding. She was breathing. It was shallow, but at least she was breathing. I called 911 and ran to get Lizzie. Later at the hospital, Mother was awake but incoherent. She didn't know who I was, and I don't think she even knew who *she* was. She continued to deny it was an overdose; she said she'd had a nervous breakdown. I didn't buy that. The social worker didn't let us linger at the hospital long, so we were carted off not knowing if Mother was going to live or die. Mother told me later she spent three days in the hospital.

I spent five days in a group home waiting for a foster home. Foster homes suck, but that group home was horrible. Mother did the crime and I did the time. That seemed to be how it went. It was the loneliest I'd ever felt. I grieved for the mother I'd once known and for Lizzie. I worried so much about Lizzie. She was so small. I was in my first foster home for two months when I found out I had an ulcer. My foster mother told me it was probably from worrying so much. I got to see Mother two times and Lizzie once while I was in foster care that time. It was the longest eight months of my life. Mother was really bad about not showing up to see us. We would be sitting at the Family Center waiting on her and she wouldn't show. Heck, most of the time she didn't even call to say why she wasn't going to be there. The social worker would just check her off as a no-show and cart us off, back to the foster home.

Interrupting my thoughts, Lizzie came running into the bedroom to let me know the pancakes were done. I told her I was fine and that she could eat the ones Mother had made for me. She shrugged her shoulders and said, "Whatever."

I followed her out into the kitchen and helped her up onto a stool at the bar. As mad as I was at my mother, I couldn't help but be happy for Lizzie. She was ecstatic that we are all together again. For her sake, I hoped it would stay that way, but I had little faith that it would. I never should have talked Mother up as much as I had to Lizzie. I was going to be sorry about that. I just knew it.

Mother looked my way and said, "Are you sure you don't want any pancakes, Jane? They're your favorite: apple cinnamon."

"No, I'm good," I replied sarcastically.

"Jane, I understand you're upset with me. I get that. But I cannot walk on eggshells the entire time we're together. Could you at least try to tone down the sarcasm for your sister's sake? Quit acting like such a child, Jane. You're fifteen years old. Start acting it."

"Sure," I mumbled.

I woke up the next morning glad it was Saturday and that I didn't have to start the dreadful hick school yet. I was sure it would be filled with farm-friendly people, especially if the boy I'd seen yesterday was any indication of how "friendly" they were. The disgust on his face when he looked at Mother's car was all I needed to know. Maybe I was being judgmental, but I'd earned the right to be a little cynical. The boy had pulled out of the driveway very fast yesterday. Someone needed to let him know there was a four-year-old around and he would need to be more careful. I didn't care if this was his house. He could be a little more considerate of other people. I was sure he was just as self-centered as he looked driving that brand-new sports car. I didn't care. It wasn't like we'd be there that long anyway.

Off to farm school

The alarm clock started blaring at 6 a.m.

Ugh, it's Monday morning already, I thought. I was not looking forward to going to a new school again. I was getting pretty good at it, though. I kept to myself, didn't attract attention, and didn't make friends. That's how to survive multiple schools during your high school years.

Mother had informed me that the school was called Whitman High School. I couldn't believe it: The school was named after that arrogant boy! That was just freaking wonderful. I didn't understand how she'd ended up being the maid to the richest family in Adams County anyway. There must not have been many options since Adams County was one of the poorest counties in the state of Ohio. I just couldn't wait to check out Whitman High School.

I figured I'd better get dressed so I could go get tortured for the day. I did finally give in and unpack my clothes. I'd decided that once they were washed, I really wouldn't want to shove them down into my backpack again. I needed one of those backpacks for school anyway. I went to the closet to find something to wear. I didn't have much to choose from, so it wasn't a hard decision. I never really cared what I looked like anyway, so it really didn't matter that I didn't have a huge wardrobe. I grabbed a black, vintage Led Zeppelin T-shirt, a pair of skinny jeans, my only necklace, my black bracelet, and my Chucks. I couldn't leave home without my Chucks. They were so old. I'd gotten them for Christmas three years ago; they were the only things I'd gotten that year. I was going to have to wear a jacket, too, because it was cold. I couldn't wait for it to get warm; I hated the cold.

I took a quick look in the mirror to make sure I didn't have boogers hanging out of my nose or anything. I brushed through my hair one more time really quickly before I headed into the kitchen. Mother always told me when I was younger that I had the blackest hair she'd ever seen. It is pretty dark; I'm lucky to have a darker complexion also. That must have come from my father's side, because Mother is pretty fair-skinned. My blue eyes stick out like a sore thumb with my black hair. I try to keep my hair grown out over my eyes. It's a nice shield when you want to hide. It was shorter than I would have liked, though, because one of the girls at my next-to-last foster home had decided to cut it when I was sleeping. It had been really long too. The only thing they could do to fix it was pretty much shave it off. I really thought I could have hurt that girl. But she got sent to the group home for it, so that would have to do. My hair was finally growing a little. I was starting to look a little more like Joan Jett instead of G.I. Jane.

I went into the kitchen, grabbed an oatmeal bar out of the cabinet, and headed for the end of the lane. I'd never had to ride a school bus in the city. I had no idea what it was like; however, I did know what it was like to ride a metro bus. I hoped the two would be similar and I would be totally ignored on this bus as well.

I was out there at the end of the lane for about five minutes when I heard the roar of that Mustang come to life. It wasn't long before the car came toward where I was standing. That boy was in the driver's seat and there was a girl in the passenger seat. Did he have a sister? It had to be his sister. Great, there were two of them. The girl glared at me as they went by. The boy just kept his eyes focused on the road and made a left out of the lane. Not long after they pulled away, the bus came. As soon as I climbed onto the bus, the worst smell hit me smack in the face. *What in the world could that be?* It smelled like some kind of crap. How disgusting!

As soon as I got to the top of the steps and turned to start down the aisle, I realized it was very quiet and everyone was staring at me. It was so humiliating. I looked around hoping to find an empty seat. Great—there wasn't one. This wasn't going to be good. Where would I sit? I started scanning people's faces looking for someone who looked a little friendly or maybe a little dorky. Someone like that might not fuss too much about me sitting with them. I saw an empty seat next to a boy with big, dark glasses, buzzed red hair, freckles, and two abnormally large front teeth. That was where I decided to sit. I walked down the aisle and took my seat next to him. He turned toward me with the strangest look. I gave him a very fake smile and said, "Hello."

He turned his head away from me and said, "They're staring at you because you're new. They don't like new. You look a little different too. That's not going to help you any. Sitting with me really just took down your chances of social survival. If you move now, you still might have a shot at it."

Wow, that was not what I'd expected him to say! "Hi" would have sufficed. I'd managed to put myself in an awkward situation within five seconds of getting on the bus. I was a genius. I had to wonder what I would do to myself by the end of the day.

"I really don't care about social survival. I probably won't be here long anyway," I replied.

He crossed his arms in front of his chest and grunted, "Whatever."

The bus ride seemed to take forever. At least the quiet hadn't lasted very long. As soon as the bus started moving again, everyone started talking. The staring didn't stop, though. I got looks all the way to school. Did I really look so different from everyone that they needed to stare at me? I didn't see anyone on the bus who was dressed like me. It's not like I had chains hanging from my pants or multiple tattoos. I thought I was dressed pretty normally. Plenty of people dressed like me in the city, and we were only an hour away. It couldn't be that different.

Several people on the bus were wearing the same kind of blue jackets. They had the letters FFA on the back, but I had no idea what it stood for until I was getting off the bus and got a closer look at one of the jackets. It said "Future Farmers of America." Too freaking funny! Are you kidding me? There was some kind of club for future farmers? Not to knock anybody who wanted to learn about farming; it was probably a lucrative business in that area. But I couldn't help but laugh out loud. This was going to be interesting.

The school wasn't very big, but it did look like it was fairly new. Mother had already registered me so I just needed to find the office and pick up my schedule. I followed all the other kids to the front entrance. Once inside, I looked around to find the office to my left. There were two ladies at a long counter. One was an older, heavy-set lady who looked to be in her sixties. She had her salt-and-pepper hair pulled up in a bun on the back of her head. The other woman was maybe in her thirties and had a small build and brown hair cut in that trendy short bob that everybody was wearing. I walked up to the counter and asked for my schedule. The younger woman asked me my name, shuffled around some papers, and handed me my schedule. She asked if I needed help getting around, and I told her no. I didn't really want to walk around with a tour guide. The school wasn't that big; I was pretty sure I could manage. She said okay and told me where the main areas were. The library was upstairs and the cafeteria was to the right of the office. She gave me a hall pass for being late, and I thanked her and headed to my first class.

I had algebra first thing. Great! That sounded like real fun first thing in the morning. My schedule said algebra was in room 202 so I figured that had to be upstairs. I walked up the stairs and headed to the left. I looked at a few of the doors and realized the numbers were going the wrong way so I turned around and headed the other direction. I found room 202 at the end of the hall. The classroom door was shut. I didn't know if I should knock or just walk in. I decided I would charge right in.

I entered the room and the teacher stopped lecturing. "Can I help you, Miss?" he asked.

I handed him my pass and showed him my schedule. He didn't say anything; he just walked over to a cabinet, opened it, and pulled out an algebra book. Handing me the book, he asked, "It's really late in the school year; are you going to be able to keep up?"

I shrugged my shoulders and answered, "I hope so."

The truth was I was no good at any kind of math and had done horribly in algebra class at my last school. I probably wouldn't do worth a crap in this one either.

The teacher told me to find a seat and that his name was Mr. McDonald. Right after he said his name, there came a "Moo!" and an "Oink!" from the back of the room. It took me a few minutes to figure out they were making fun of his name and not me. Of course Old McDonald would teach at the farm school in cow country. That made perfect sense. Once I got done laughing to myself, I looked around to find a seat. I didn't have to look far. The only empty seat was in the front row. I had no choice. That's where I was going to be stuck for the rest of the school year.

After almost an hour of learning about the slope of a line, I was so ready to head to my next class. I really needed to find my locker since I would soon have a nice stack of books. Most of the lockers were upstairs, so I was sure I could find it. My locker number was 420. Of course it was. Everything else in my life revolved around drugs, so why not my locker too? I got lucky and found it pretty quickly. Then, I was off to search for my next class, psychology, which sounded even more fun than algebra.

I fumbled around the school for the rest of the morning until it was time for lunch. Mother had made sure to sign me up for free lunches, so I would get to humiliate myself in the lunch line. I was used to it. I'd always gotten free lunches when I was in foster care. I shoved all my stuff except for my jacket in my locker and headed toward the cafeteria. The cafeteria was pretty full already. I took my place in line behind two girls who had very long hair and wore skirts down to their ankles. I must have missed the memo on that one. They turned around, gave me a once-over, and went back to their chatter. After going to so many schools in the past few years, I should have been used to all the strange looks, but I wasn't. I really wished I were invisible. It would have been nice to go through life totally unnoticed. Probably wouldn't have been any disappointments that way. I knew I had to learn to stop having expectations of people. If I had no expectations of anyone, then they couldn't disappoint me. That would be my new motto. I liked that: No more expectations.

I finally made it up to get my food. I chose to eat pizza. I could have lived on pizza; I *had* lived on pizza. Hot, cold, stale, or moldy, it didn't matter. Lizzie and I had eaten a lot of pizza the last time we'd lived with Mother. Our apartment was above a pizza restaurant and I think the manager knew we were alone a lot because she was always sending up pizzas that were supposedly made wrong.

I got to the register and the lady asked for my lunch number. I knew I'd seen it on my schedule. I started searching my pockets when I realized I'd put my schedule in my notepad. Crap. I didn't have a dime on me to pay for my food. I told the lady I was new and my lunch number was in my locker. She told me it was my problem and to pay for my food or get out of the line. Wow—no sympathy from her. She was rude. I was getting ready to put my tray back on top of the counter when someone reached around me and handed the lady two bucks. I turned to see who it was. It was Mustang Boy. More charity—that was just wonderful.

"That's okay, really. I'm not hungry anyway. Keep your money," I urged.

"It's no big deal; you can pay me back later. Besides, I know where you live," he said, chuckling.

I set the tray on the counter. "No, I don't want it," I snapped.

"Now, you two are going to have to make up your minds, Landon. I don't have all day," the lady said.

Mustang Boy grinned at her and said, "Keep it, Mabel. Look how puny she is. I think she needs to eat something, don't you?"

I grabbed the tray and took off toward the tables.

"Whatever. Thanks."

As I was walking away, I heard Mabel say something about me being "a snippy little thing." Then I heard Mustang Boy laugh out loud. I sure was glad he'd amused himself at my expense.

I looked around for a place to sit. *Please let me find an empty table.* I did not want to sit with anyone. I looked around and found an empty table over in the corner by the stage. I sat down facing the stage so I wouldn't have to see everyone staring at me. The gawking was really getting ridiculous. For some reason, people here didn't seem to mind getting busted staring. They just keep right on looking. It was crazy. I sat there the entire lunch period with my back to them so I didn't have to watch. After lunch, I went about the rest of the day with my head down, trying to avoid all the stares.

I was so happy for my first day to be over. The day had gone pretty well except for my run-in with Mustang Boy. I still couldn't believe he'd done that. I wondered if his family would be keeping track of how much they did for my family. They could log everything to see if their little charity experiment was working. I could offer to start them a spreadsheet. I so hated this. The day could have been worse, though. The best part was that no one had tried to talk to me. I didn't need anyone trying to be my friend. Sure, I got looks, but I always did. It was more than usual, but at least no one had tried to buddy up to me. Usually when they did that, they were just trying to get the scoop on me. I'd never give it up, though, so eventually they'd quit trying. Besides, who knew how long I'd be there anyway?

Lizzie was watching her tablet when I got home. SpongeBob and Hannah Montana were the only two shows she watched. She also couldn't seem to get enough of JoJo Siwa YouTube videos. She'd rarely gotten to watch what she wanted when we were in the foster homes, so she was living it up. And that tablet—Mother had scored big points with Lizzie when she'd bought her that thing. Mother was gathering up laundry so she and Lizzie could go to the laundromat. We didn't have a washer or dryer in our tiny house.

While they were gone, I had tried to work on homework, but the only thing I got accomplished was reading the chapter on addiction in my psychology book. It wasn't the assigned chapter to read, but I was obsessed with reading anything to do with addiction. I guess it was my way of trying to understand why Mother loved drugs more than she loved me and Lizzie. No matter what I read, I never found the answer to the question that haunted me. When I was first placed into foster care, I got every book on addiction I could find in the library. They all said the same thing: that she did love me and that her addiction was about her and not me. And that addiction was a disease. I had a hard time with that one. People don't choose to have cancer, but they do choose to stick a needle in their arm. That was my theory anyway. She'd chosen to keep herself so doped up she couldn't take care of us anymore. She'd chosen to stay gone for days at a time. She'd chosen to sell everything we owned. It was all her choice and now I was just supposed to forgive her and act like none of that had happened, just look over all of it because she was sick. I couldn't do it. I wouldn't do it.

At suppertime, Mother insisted we all sit at the breakfast counter together. Our little house was too small for a kitchen table, so Mother had bought three stools for the counter. She said she wanted to have family time. She was laying it on thick. I would do what she wanted for Lizzie's sake, but I would not believe it would last. Nothing ever lasted. I quietly picked at my supper, hit the shower, and went to bed.

I pretty much lived in solitude for the next month. I went to school and just did what I had to do. It seemed like every school I went to had one of those crowds of girls who think they are so much better than everyone else. They are always superficially pretty and downright mean. And for some reason, those crowds always tried to single me out. Mustang Boy's sister, Emily, belonged to the clique at this school. I thought she might have been the head bitch. I'd been getting some notes taped to the front of my locker and I was pretty sure those girls were behind it. They always said something like "skank," "white trash," or "freak." That showed how mature they were. I just tore them down and went on. For the most part, people had stopped gawking at me so much. Hopefully the newness was wearing off and they would just let me be invisible—minus the nice little love notes, of course. I didn't think that would stop until they got some kind of reaction from me. They wanted to tick me off until I went off on them and looked like a freaking lunatic. I wouldn't give them the satisfaction. They didn't mean anything to me. I'd taught myself a long time ago to keep to myself and not to expect anything good out of anybody.

Tornado warning and the witch

I awoke on a Saturday morning in early April with a weird feeling in the pit of my stomach. It was a gloomy day and I somehow had managed to sleep until eleven. I must have been really tired. I could hear Lizzie belting out JoJo Siwa from the living room. I decided I would be bright and cheery just for her today. I strolled into the living room singing the words to her favorite song.

She giggled, saying, "Jane, you so silly! You don't like JoJo Siwa."

"Nope, but I sure do like to hear you laugh, Lizzie Lou," I replied.

She sat down on the couch with the Easter basket she'd gotten from the Easter Bunny last Sunday and started munching.

"Jane, what are we going to do today? Do you have school?" she asked.

I sat down beside her and stole a Reese's Egg from her basket.

"No, it's Saturday; I don't have school today. What would you like to do?" I replied.

"I want to go fishing in that pond by the barn," she answered.

I burst out laughing.

"Fishing! Are you crazy? We don't know how to fish."

"But Jane, SpongeBob goes jellyfishing all the time and he's not that smart. It can't be that tough," she explained.

Sometimes I'd forget she was only four when she talked like that. She was so smart. I told her we might try to go some other time; it was too wet outside to do much of anything.

Mother came out of the bathroom freshly showered. She informed me she had made some friends at her Narcotics Anonymous meeting and they were going to go to the bowling alley in Hillsboro. Here we go! She'd done well to stay home with us for a month before she wanted to start going out again. And of course, the first thing that went through my mind was that this couldn't be good if she'd met her friends at NA. That meant they were addicts too.

"Jane, is that okay with you? Do you mind to stay with Lizzie while I'm out?" Mother asked.

"I don't care. It's not like I'm going anywhere," I replied.

She started in with the "You do need to make some friends" lecture in which she'd tell me I spent way too much time by myself or with Lizzie and that I really needed to be around people my own age. She had no clue how different I was from most people my own age. I'd endured a good bit because of the likes of her and I would never fit in with my "peers" now. Not that I wanted to conform to what society expected of me anyway. According to society, I should have been giggling over guys, shopping for dresses in the hopes of getting asked to the prom, or even worse, trying out for the cheerleading squad. Nope, no thank you.

The rest of the day was uneventful. I showered, Mother made an early supper, and Lizzie played in the house all day. We'd been here a month and she was still trying to be Mommy of the Year. She cooked, she cleaned, she went to work, she played with Lizzie, and she even made multiple attempts to talk to me. But I wasn't getting my hopes up that we could be some happy family. As soon as I did, she would screw it up again. She'd already started to ruin it by going out with her so-called friends.

Mother headed out for the bowling alley around 7:30. Lizzie and I settled down in the living room to watch a DVD. We were about halfway into the movie when the phone rang. It was Mother. She said she'd heard on the radio there was a tornado warning one county over and the storms were headed in our direction. She insisted we go to the Whitmans' house and ask if we could stay in their basement until the storms passed. I tried to argue with her to let us stay in our house, but she wouldn't budge. When had she gotten so "motherly"? I was starting to feel like I was in the Twilight Zone. I surrendered; it wasn't worth the effort. And besides, if the weather was going to be that bad, I would want Lizzie to be in a safe place. I told Mother we'd go over to the Whitmans' right away.

This was just great. It was bad enough I had to deal with Landon and Emily Whitman at school, but to be in their house— yuck! I hadn't spoken to Mustang Boy since my first day of school. Still, I got Lizzie's shoes and jacket on her, and she asked why we were going to the Whitmans' house. I told her it was going to storm and a basement was one of the safest places to be.

As we knocked on the back door, the wind was really picking up. The sound of Mrs. Whitman's wind chimes was creepy; the chimes were whipping around in every direction. We stood there for a few minutes before Landon came to the door, wearing sweats and a tank—the kind of tank people refer to as a "wife-beater." He wasn't dressed at all like any other time I'd seen him. At school, he always wore Hollister and Nike. Not that I'd been keeping track of what he was wearing at school, but I liked to people watch. I could tell you a good bit about a lot of people from school even though I'd never spoken to any of them.

Landon looked me directly in the eye and asked if he could help us. I quickly looked away and down to the ground.

"I hate to bother you," I said, "but my mother isn't home and she called insisting that we ask to stay in your basement. I guess there's a really bad storm coming. If it's too much of an inconvenience for you, we can go back to the house."

He started rubbing the back of his head and said, "Actually, my mom called me too and told me to come ask your family if you'd like to use our basement. I'm going to head down there myself. I guess it's a pretty bad storm. My dad is away on business and Mom and Emily are in Cincinnati visiting friends for the night. Come on in. I'll go find a flashlight and a few other things to take down with us."

He took off through the kitchen.

"The door to the basement is through that hall to the left, third door down. You can go on and get settled if you'd like. I'll meet you there in a few minutes."

"Okay, thank you," I replied.

Why was he being so nice to us? I'd been so rude to him last month and he hadn't tried to talk to me again since that day. Any time I was near him, I thought about that first day I saw him in his car or that first day of school and felt as if he looked down on me, like he was better than me because he had money and I didn't.

As we walked to the basement door, I noticed there were pictures hanging all through the hallway, pictures of Landon and Emily from the time they were babies up until the present. I could have lingered and looked at them all, but I knew Landon would be back soon and I didn't want to get caught snooping. I doubted Mother still had pictures of us from when we were babies. I had managed to hold on to a few of Lizzie.

We opened the door, found a light switch along the wall, and headed down the stairs. The basement looked its age. It was not bright and shiny like the rest of the house. It was cold, dark, and downright creepy.

Lizzie squeezed my hand tightly as we walked farther down the stairs.

"Jane, I a little afraid," she whispered.

"Don't worry, Lizzie, it's not that bad," I reassured her. "We're only going to stay down here until the storms are gone, okay?"

We found a couple of old lawn chairs in the back corner of the basement. I grabbed them and pulled them closer to the stairs, because I did not want to make Lizzie sit in the back of that creepy room.

Landon came down the stairs carrying a bag, a few blankets, a flashlight, and a radio. Evidently he'd done this before.

He looked our way and said, "I see you found the chairs. I have some blankets here if you get cold and some snacks in case you girls get hungry."

"Thanks. You really didn't have to go to all that trouble. Hopefully the storm will pass over quickly and we can get out of your way," I replied.

Landon walked over to a fold-out table that was set up along the wall, set the radio down, and started putting fresh batteries in it. I couldn't help but stare at him while he was messing with the radio. He was quite gorgeous. He was probably about six feet tall and he was thin. Not thin enough to look gangly and awkward; he was filled out nicely. He had muscular arms and his chest looked as hard as a rock. He looked so engulfed in his task that I didn't think he would catch me staring. For some reason, I couldn't help myself. His hair was a light brown with some lighter streaks through it. It was grown out like most guys were wearing their hair then, that longer shag look. His eyes were such a deep brown that they resembled the color of chocolate. I'd noticed those the moment Landon had looked at me when he answered the door.

I heard the radio come to life and looked away quickly, but not quickly enough. I'm pretty sure he caught me gawking at him. The thunder was growing very loud, and I could tell Lizzie was getting a little anxious. I grabbed one of the blankets, wrapped her in it, and held her cradled in my lap.

"Jane, will Mommy be okay in the storm?" she asked.

"She will be just fine. I'm sure she's in a safe place."

Then, Lizzie looked up at me and asked, "Is she going to come back, Jane? Last time she never came back. I don't want to go live with other families again. I like it here."

"As long as it's me and you kid, that's all that matters, okay?" I responded.

What was I supposed to tell her? That everything would be okay and we would never have to go live with other families again? She was only four. I couldn't very well tell her the complete truth, but I sure didn't want to tell her bald faced lies about our future either. We had Mother for that.

Lizzie was looking very sleepy when she said, "Jane, will the storm drop off the witch?"

I chuckled and answered, "No, Lizzie. That's one thing I'm sure of. No witches will be dropped off here tonight."

I looked up to see what Landon was doing. He was sitting in one of the lawn chairs about six feet away and was looking right at us. He didn't look away when I caught him staring.

You could see the lightning flashing outside the little windows at the top of the basement walls. Hail starting pounding the sides of the house; it was very loud. The radio was reporting a tornado that was spotted in Russellville and was headed east. I didn't know enough about the area to know that meant it was headed in our direction. We sat there quietly listening to the storm for a while. Lizzie had managed to fall asleep in my arms.

I was startled when Landon spoke to me.

"Jane, I couldn't help but overhear you talking to Lizzie," he said. "Is that why you're rude all the time and don't talk to anybody at school? Do you think you won't be here long?"

"What are you talking about?" I snapped at him.

Was he really going to do this? Why would he care who I talked to at school? And how would he even know if I talked to anybody at school or not? Was he keeping tabs on me?

Landon continued his questions.

"Why is Lizzie worried that your mother won't come back? Has she done that to you before?"

"Did anyone ever tell you eavesdropping is wrong and you shouldn't do it?" I asked, scowling.

He looked at me with confusion on his face.

"Why do you do that? I only asked you a question because I'm curious about you, but you treat me like I've done something to offend you."

"So, you're curious about the girl from the gutter who somehow ended up in the middle of cow country. I'm sure you've heard enough to put it together. Here, I'll give you the short version: 'Mom messes up; kids are taken away. Mom gets kids back; mom messes up again; kids are taken away again. Mom must have slept with the judge to get kids back again. Mom and kids end up in the middle of nowhere. The end.' Does that satisfy your curiosity? Now you can tell all your pretentious friends about your mother's charity-case family and maybe everyone will stop staring at me all the time."

"That's why you think I'm curious, so I can run to school and tell everyone all about you?" Landon responded. "And is that how you perceive me, as pretentious? I'm not the one walking around with a chip on my shoulder refusing to acknowledge anyone in the world around them. I can't help but to watch you with Lizzie. Your demeanor is so different from the way you are with anyone else. I also hear the way you talk about your mother with disgust. I was curious about what she could have done to make you despise her so much. I'm naturally a curious person and I'm sorry if my interest in you has offended you. Don't take it personally. I'm always curious about the people around me."

"Haven't you ever heard curiosity killed the cat?" I asked.

"I try to explain myself to you and you still snap at me. Do you enjoy sarcasm?" he demanded with a half-cocked grin on his face.

I couldn't tell if he was being serious or goading me. Either way, he was ticking me off.

"Don't sit down here and judge me," I hissed. "I saw you pull out of the garage the day we moved in. You looked at my mother's car with disgust, like we weren't good enough to be your family's employee, let alone live next to you in your servants' quarters."

I was getting very upset. This boy who had everything he could possibly want was getting his kicks out of rattling my cage.

"Is that what you think of me, that I would judge someone by their car?" Landon asked. "I must really give a bad first impression. I wasn't judging you or your car. I had just had an argument with my sister. She was standing beside the barn out past your car. You couldn't have seen her from the window you were looking out of. And for your information, you're not my mother's charity case. Every one of her housekeepers has lived in that little house. It's a small house, not servants' quarters. We aren't living in an eighteenth-century novel, Jane. Mom is pretty demanding. She likes to have her employees close in case she needs anything. Jax, the groundskeeper, lives up the road at the other end of our property. Mom has gone through quite a few housekeepers and groundskeepers."

I felt like he was telling me the truth, but who knows and why did it even matter? He was nothing to me. I did feel bad for judging him so quickly, though. Being judgmental was not a quality I liked in other people, but apparently I was getting pretty good at it myself. I took a deep breath and sighed.

"I'm sorry," I mumbled. "I had no right to judge you. You've been very nice to us tonight and I shouldn't have been so impolite."

Being wrong was one thing, but admitting it was something altogether different. It was like asking for help when you're determined to do something on your own. Asking for help was another thing I rarely did.

"That's okay," Landon said. "I get that a lot."

I could see the smirk on his face as he sat there looking at me.

"You look awfully smug. Did you enjoy that?" I asked.

He started laughing and flipped his chair up and around so it was next to mine. He ran his hand across my forehead and asked, "Do you realize that when you get angry, you get this line across here that gives you away?"

I flinched from his touch. I did not expect him to touch me. Lizzie was the only person who'd been in my personal space in a long time. Landon made me nervous. There was something about the way his brown eyes looked at me that made me look away. My stomach started to ball up in a knot and I could feel my face getting red.

"I think the storm is over now," I said. "We must have escaped the worst of it. We should get back to the house now."

Landon smiled.

"I'm pretty sure it's been over for a while now," he said. "You probably would have realized that had you not been scolding me."

"I was not scolding you!" I argued.

"Watch out—your line is starting to show," Landon said, chuckling.

I got out of my chair and stomped off toward the stairs. "You're really starting to irritate me," I complained.

"Would you like me to carry her for you?" he asked, nodding at Lizzie. "Those stairs are pretty steep."

I normally would not have agreed, but he was right: The stairs were steep and I did not want to take the chance of falling with my sister in my arms.

"Thank you," I growled.

Landon reached out to take Lizzie from me. I didn't know how she would have reacted if she'd awakened and seen he was carrying her. Lizzie never met a stranger, so she probably wouldn't have cared. Landon lifted her from me and headed for the stairs. I followed behind him. It was still raining outside, but not nearly as badly as it had been earlier.

When we got to our house, I opened the door and pointed Landon toward our room. I showed him which bed to put Lizzie in and he laid her down gently. She rolled over onto her side and tucked her little hands under her pillow. I took her shoes off, pulled the covers over her, and walked into the living room.

Landon already had walked back to the door and was getting ready to walk outside when he turned to me and said, "I do have one question, if you don't mind."

I leaned up against the wall, crossed my arms, looked directly at him, and said, "Oh yeah, what would that be?"

He stifled a laugh. "Why on earth would Lizzie think that storm was going to drop off a witch?"

I couldn't help but crack a smile.

"We were watching *The Wizard of Oz* before we came to your house," I answered.

Landon chuckled as he walked out the door.

What had happened tonight? Why was he being nice to me? I was nothing to him. But I ended up dreaming of that boy all night long.

I woke the next morning and still couldn't believe Landon had gotten into my space the way he had. When he touched my face, I thought I was going to freak out. The feeling I got in the pit of my stomach was unlike anything I'd ever felt before. I still didn't understand why he'd done that. He hadn't made another attempt to talk to me since my first day of school when I had seen him in the lunch room.

He was definitely not what I'd thought he was. I'd had him pegged as this arrogant ass and he actually seemed like a pretty nice guy. I'd noticed before that he was nice-looking, but now I seemed to be very aware that he was absolutely gorgeous and I couldn't get him off my mind. I'd never really thought of him that way before. I guess I just couldn't see past what I'd thought was arrogance.

Freaky lunch friends

It was Monday again, time to head back to Farm School. It was pretty much a normal day, until lunch. I hadn't seen Landon all day, so when I hit the lunch room I looked around to see if I could find him, not that I would have approached him anyway. He could have just been being nice to me because we were neighbors. Yeah, that's all it was. I put my head down and went through the line, grabbed my pizza, and headed to my table in the corner. I sat with my back toward the rest of the cafeteria the way I always did. I was just starting to enjoy my pizza when some girl I'd never seen before came over to my table, set her tray down, and claimed a seat. She was a pretty girl. She was thin and kind of tall, and her hair hung in red ringlets that fell just below her shoulders. Her red hair had blonde highlights in it and the curls were loose. She was wearing a T-shirt that said, "Life's a Beach."

"Do you mind if I sit with you?" she asked. "I hate new schools and I just never know where to sit. Ya know, I went to a new school back home and ended up sittin' down right smack in the middle of the snotty girls. I sure don't wanna do that again. They were so dang mean to me. I was glad I only had to go to that school a month before we moved again. So, I'm figurin' since you're sittin' by yourself that you must be new too. My name is Milah Jo, and I just moved here from Alabama. We just got up here yesterday and Mama's already makin' me go to school. Do you believe that? She didn't even let me get all my stuff unpacked. We moved up here 'cause my mama done got tired of my daddy runnin' around all the time. She said she wasn't gonna put up with it no more and packed us kids right up in Daddy's Chevette. Boy, I bet he was mad when he found out his car was gone. Anyway, Mama brought us young'uns up here to live with Maw and Paw. We may be here a few days or a few months. I just never know anymore. Did I tell you my name is Milah Jo? What's yours, hon?"

Um, okay. This was strange. I hadn't asked her to sit with me and I sure hadn't asked for her life story, but she'd given it to me anyway. How should I deal with this one? I so knew what it is like to be the new kid. She couldn't mean any harm because she didn't know anyone yet, right?

"I'm Jane, Jane Michaels," I answered. "Yes, I'm new. I've been here about a month."

"Girl, you been here a month and you're still sittin' by yourself? What, do you not make friends easy? Smell bad or something? Oh gosh, you brush your teeth, don't ya? Cause that's just nasty if you don't. How in the world could you be here a month and not have any friends? My mama tells me I'm a social butterfly and I will bloom wherever I go. She also tells me I never know when to shut up neither. She thinks I just rattle on and on all the time."

Then, Milah Jo laughed, very loudly. I didn't laugh with her.

All I could think about was how that laugh would be drawing attention our way. I decided I was going to have to get rid of her.

"I hate to tell you, Milah Jo, but I'm not well-liked here, and sitting with me may be social suicide. So if you want to be a social butterfly, you might want to find another place to sit."

She gave me a strange look.

"Hon, I make friends wherever I go. I make enemies too. And my senses tell me you need a friend, so unless you wanna be mean and run me off, you'll let me sit with you for a little while. But of course, darlin', if I'm really botherin' ya, I can move."

Okay, now I felt like an ass. I didn't want to intentionally be mean to anyone. And she sounded so genuine with that Southern accent of hers. I figured it wouldn't hurt to let her sit with me at lunch until she made some friends.

"If you want to sit here, I guess you can," I finally said.

"Thanks, hon, that sure is nice of you. So, can you fill me in on any of the good gossip about any of the students here?"

"As you can see, I sit alone, so I don't know much of anything about anybody around here. You'll have to go scouting around somewhere else to get that info," I explained.

The truth was I might not have talked to anybody, but I sure did observe them. You could learn a lot from observation. I was pretty sure Emily was Queen Bee of the snotty girls and that there were a bunch of guys so into farming that they were in a club for it. I didn't know what to think of the girls with the long hair and long skirts. The jury was still out on that one.

Before Milah Jo had a chance to say anything, a tray landed on the other side of mine. What the hell was going on today? I turned and looked up to see Landon standing there.

"I see you're letting people sit with you today and I thought I would join in while I had the chance. Do you mind?" he asked.

This had to be some kind of joke. Why couldn't these people just leave me alone already?

"You're kidding me, right?" I said. "Why would you even want to sit with me?"

"Girl, what in the world are you doin'?" Milah Jo chimed in. "Come on over here, honey. You can sit next to me. I don't mind," she said, patting the seat next to her.

"That's really nice of you. And what is your name?" Landon asked her.

"Oh, my name is Milah Jo. Milah Jo Duncan. And your name is?"

I was pretty sure she was starting to drool.

Landon reached out his hand to shake Milah Jo's.

"Nice to meet you. I'm Landon Whitman. If you don't mind, I'd like to take this seat next to Jane."

"That's fine, hon. You sit wherever you like as long as it's at this table," Milah Jo said. "I would have to say that Landon Whitman sounds like a fine, upstanding name. Suits you well, I think."

What was Landon doing? Didn't he realize everyone was going to see him sitting with me?

"Aren't you worried that someone might see you over here?" I asked. "I'm sure you've heard all the stuff they say about me."

That was my one last plea to get him to move. Deep down, I really didn't want him to go. For some reason, I craved his company now, but I sure didn't want him to know that. No matter how much I wanted him to sit with me, I had to get him to leave.

He raised his eyebrows and cocked a grin.

"Really, Jane, are you judging me again? I don't care what they see and I don't believe what they say. I told you the other night that I'm not like that. I meant it. You've sparked my curiosity and I would really like to get to know you if that's okay."

Milah Jo leaned over my way and spoke what I think she thought was a whisper, but I'm sure Landon and everyone else in the cafeteria heard her.

"Girl, if you don't tell that boy what he wants to know about you, I'm gonna tell him everything he could possibly ever want to know about *me*. That boy is HOT! Woo, Wee! HOT!"

I could feel my face turning red. I had known this girl for maybe ten minutes and she had already managed to embarrass me. Instead of shrinking down in my chair like I normally did, I decided I would try to act like I had some kind of confidence.

"Are you curious about me, Landon, or the story behind me?" I snapped.

"You got a story behind ya, girlie?" Milah Jo interrupted. "You better start spillin', toots. I'm always up for a good story."

"No, there's no story here," I said, sighing.

"Jane, I would just really like to get to know you. That's it," Landon said.

He leaned in close to my face.

"I like you. You're not like all the other girls around here. They're all so superficial. You seem real. With you, what you see is what you get. I like that. Can't we be friends?"

How was I to respond to that? I'd gone so long avoiding any kind of interaction with other people, I didn't even know if I would know how to be somebody's friend. Now all of a sudden I had two people sitting next to me claiming they wanted to be my friends. They both seemed genuine too. I'd decided long ago I wouldn't open myself up to get hurt, but I was so lonely. The only person I ever actually carried on a conversation with was four years old. Maybe I could just pretend to be friends with them. I didn't have to expose my whole, real self to them. Okay, it would be nice to have somebody to sit with at lunch or go do something with every once in a while. Oh, no. No. No. No. I couldn't be considering this. This was not a good idea. I knew it wouldn't end well, yet I couldn't bring myself to turn them away. It was so lonely being me.

"I guess since the both of you have decided to invade my space and declare it Jane Needs a Friend Day, I guess I could give you both a chance. But, don't expect much from me. I will not be a good friend," I advised.

Milah Jo smiled big and clapped her hands together.

"Darlin', I told you I make friends wherever I go. So what are we doing this weekend?"

"You want to do something this weekend? Well, you're probably going to have to ask someone else about that, because I don't know anything about this place or what they do here in Hicksville," I replied.

Milah Jo smiled at me again and then pointed straight at Landon.

He was leaning back in his chair with a huge grin on his face.

"That works for me. What are you girls up for?"

"I don't know. What do farm kids do around here?" I queried.

"We farm kids here in Hicksville do a lot of things. Some probably aren't so different from what you did in the city. Others will probably sound crazy to you, City Girl. I bet you don't even have it in you to keep up. Do you want to do something you're used to or something you've never done before? Or are you scared?"

Now he was just looking totally full of himself.

I dropped my pizza onto my plate.

"I can take anything you throw at me, Mustang Boy!"

I've always been secretly competitive; I don't like for someone to think I can't do something. I didn't know if Landon somehow knew that or if he just got lucky, but either way he had my full attention.

He leaned up and folded his hands on the table. I could tell he was starting to enjoy this.

"Okay, how about a little paintball war on Saturday?" Landon suggested.

I leaned forward toward the table also.

"Is that something like laser tag? Because I'm pretty good at that."

Milah Jo burst out laughing.

"Girl, paintball ain't nothin' like laser tag! Laser tag is for sissies; paintball will hurt your ass."

She looked over at Landon.

"Dude, seriously? You say you like Jane here and you wanna take her out and shoot her up with paintballs. What the hell is that about?"

He looked at me and then looked at Milah Jo.

"Jane would be on my team; I would totally have her back. Kyle can go with us and partner up with you, Milah Jo."

I was pretty sure the twinkles in Milah Jo's eyes were spelling out "double date." There was no doubt she liked the idea of that. I would have to straighten her out to make sure she knew this was no kind of date—just a few people doing something fun. That was it.

"Sounds good to me. Just let me know when and where," I lied.

Getting shot with balls of paint did not sound good to me. But I would give it a try, especially if Landon thought I was scared.

He leaned back in his chair again.

"We can head out around ten Saturday morning to pick up Milah Jo and Kyle. Milah Jo, where do you live anyway?"

Milah Jo looked like she was going to jump right out of her chair.

"I live out on the old McCoy farm on Graces Run Road. Do you know where that is?"

How in the world was I going to be friends with this girl? Every emotion she felt just radiated from her. I didn't radiate crap.

Landon looked a little confused.

"Do you mean Otis and Thelma's place?"

Milah Jo smiled and said, "Yeah, hon, that's my Maw and Paw. Do you know 'em?"

Landon didn't look confused anymore.

"Everybody knows Otis and Thelma. I'm pretty sure you can find Otis sitting in McDonald's having his coffee every morning around six."

Milah Jo laughed.

"Yep, that's my Paw! Maw gets so mad at him. She just don't understand why he can't drink his coffee at home."

The bell rang, which meant my very freaky lunch was over. Good thing, too, because I didn't think I could have handled much more awkwardness. As we got out of our seats, Landon let us know he would see us again tomorrow at lunch and headed toward the gym. Milah Jo asked if she could see my schedule, because she wanted to know if any of our classes matched up for the rest of the day. We had English together last period. She was happy she would see a familiar face at least once throughout the rest of the day. She even told me she was "tickled pink." Who says that?

I was glad to end the day and get off that stinking-ass bus. I had to find out what that smell was. It was horrible. I took my time walking up the lane to the house. I needed time to reflect on my day. How had things gotten so strange all of a sudden? I'd really thought I'd fallen into a nice routine of solitude. It had been a month and no one had bothered to try to be my friend. I'd been doing pretty well, until now. I had to admit, though: There was a small part of me that was kind of excited at the thought of Landon wanting to get to know me. I just didn't understand why. There wasn't anything special about me. And I was not real sure what to think of Milah Jo yet. That accent of hers was so funny. She called everyone "hon" and "darlin'." She did seem like a pretty interesting person. I would have to make sure I kept my guard up. I didn't want to let these two very close to me; I would just end up hurt if I did.

It had been a really long time since I'd attempted to be someone's friend. It scared the crap out of me, but at the same time it was nice to think I would actually have someone to talk to every now and then. I didn't have to tell them anything about me or my life. Just keep it simple. That's all I had to do.

Paintball wars

The week seemed to fly by. I'd thought for sure it would drag since I was a little excited about the idea of going to do something Saturday. How had I gotten here? Hadn't I sworn off having friends altogether? I couldn't believe I'd caved. I was just so tired of being lonely. Solitude was great, but eventually I think a person gets tired of herself. Talking to Lizzie was wonderful. She was such a funny four-year-old, but I did need someone older to talk to once in a while. That didn't mean I was going to set myself up to be hurt. If I had to move in a month, I didn't want it to hurt because I'd attached myself to a couple of friends. I didn't need any more pain. I'd had enough.

Milah Jo and Landon had sat with me every day that week. We'd mostly talked about our upcoming paintball war. I never really had to say too much. Milah Jo always had plenty to talk about. She was one of the most flamboyant people I'd ever met. She was so loud and always drawing attention to herself—the opposite of me. She ended up getting a seat right next to mine in English. I'd thought it was bad to have to start a new school in March; poor Milah Jo had had to start in April.

Landon looked more gorgeous every day. It was like the more I got to know him, the sexier he became. Milah Jo was constantly grilling him with questions, so I got to learn a lot about him without having to reveal anything about myself. I needed to make sure to thank her for that. Milah Jo had pretty much given us her life story on her first day of school, so Landon hadn't asked her too many questions in return.

I learned that Landon liked to read sci-fi books, which meant he loved sci-fi movies. *Lord of the Rings* was his favorite. He also liked reality TV, played the guitar, and listened to country music and nothing else. He had told Milah Jo to chalk that one up to having been born and bred a country boy. That was going to be interesting. I did not understand how anyone listened to that "cry in my beer" stuff. Landon talked a lot about his family and how his dad was gone all the time. He really didn't know his dad that well since he'd never been around him much. He and his sister had never gotten along, and he drove Emily to school only because his mom made him. He was happy she would be getting her license soon and would start driving herself to school.

Then he apologized to me for the nice little notes I'd been getting on my locker, because he was pretty sure his sister was behind that. He told us her holier-than-thou attitude must have made her feel entitled to do whatever she wanted to do to people. He hated being considered part of one of the most prominent families in the county. He looked right at me and smiled when he said people tended to get the wrong idea about him because his family had money. Landon seemed to answer all of Milah Jo's questions with such ease and openness. I couldn't comprehend how anyone could just lay it all out there like that.

Saturday had come and I was having a hard time figuring out what to wear. The only thing Landon had told us about paintball attire was to layer, layer, layer. It was only going to be about fifty degrees, so being cold-natured, I had no problem with layers. The problem was I didn't really have that many clothes to layer. I went to the closet and started piling on clothes and ended up looking like I was about twenty pounds heavier than I was. I looked like one of those cows out in the field. The layers were supposed to take some of the sting out of getting shot by a paintball. Great—what was I supposed to layer on my face, ski masks? I didn't have any of those.

I was ready at about a quarter 'til ten. I decided to go outside and wait for Landon. I gave Lizzie a big kiss goodbye and she wished me luck. Mother asked me whether I was sure paintball was something I wanted to do. I ignored her and headed out the door as she was telling me to be careful. She was always on me about making some friends, so she hadn't pried too much when I'd told her what I would be doing.

Landon was already standing by the garage. He didn't look like he had too many layers on.

"Looks like you remembered your layers," he said, smirking. "I think it looks good on you."

"Yeah, right!" I said, nodding.

Landon shook his head. "Oh no, are we going to start with the sarcasm already this morning? May we please call a truce for the day? You really need to learn how to take a compliment, City Girl."

I walked over to where he was standing.

"I will chill with the sarcasm when you quit being so smug."

He put his hand out to shake mine.

"Deal."

I shook his hand.

"Deal."

Wow! The warmth of his hands shot a heat wave completely through my body. I could feel myself blush. What the crap? I never blushed, and there I was blushing for the second time in a week. This wasn't good. Maybe I should just back out now. I was sure once I got in that car that I wouldn't get another chance to bail. I couldn't bring myself to do it, though. I really did want to go with him.

Landon waved his other hand in front of my face.

"Uh, Jane, can I have my hand back now or were you planning on keeping it?"

I pulled my hand away from his quickly. I was definitely blushing and I knew he'd seen it. He just smiled and motioned for us to enter the garage. I knew his car was nice from seeing the outside of it, but my goodness, I sure hadn't expected the inside. It was astounding. It had heated leather seats, satellite radio, and built-in GPS. It looked more like the inside of a spaceship. I'd never been in such a nice car.

Once we pulled out of the driveway, I didn't know what to talk about. Milah Jo always broke the silence at school, but she wasn't there yet to do that. I was on my own until we picked her up. Then I realized I had no idea where she lived.

"Landon, how long will it take to get to Milah Jo's?" I asked.

We were stopped at the end of the driveway. Landon turned my way and grinned.

"Well, Milah Jo seemed pretty excited at the idea of partnering up with Kyle today, so I asked him if he would pick her up and meet us there. Is that okay? She's a really nice girl, but I never get to talk to you when she's around. That girl can talk. I was hoping we could use this time to get to know each other. Or at least me get to know you. Milah Jo has done a pretty good job of interrogating me this week. I'm guessing you know pretty much everything there is to know about me."

All of a sudden, I felt like my heart was going to jump right out of my chest. I could feel my pits and my palms getting all sweaty, yet my feet were freezing. Those were sure signs I was nervous. I was just hoping my stomach would keep it together, because that was usually what came next. This wasn't going to be good. He'd tricked me. I didn't want him to know anything about me or my sad, so-called life.

Landon went ahead and pulled out of the driveway. I had no idea where we were going. It was quiet, and I wasn't sure what to say. The only sounds were the roar of the engine and the country music playing on the stereo. It wasn't up very loud, but I could hear the man singing something about being on the porch in the backwoods. I just didn't get that music, and I couldn't help but snicker.

Landon threw a quick glance my way.

"What's so funny?"

"I just don't get this music," I replied. "Is there any meaning to any of it other than sitting on the porch because they lost their woman or their dog?"

Landon burst into a very loud laugh.

"Don't knock it until you've given it a chance," he said "It's not all about losing your woman or your dog. And what kind of music would you prefer, City Girl?"

That was a question I could answer. It wasn't too personal, and maybe it would satisfy his curiosity.

"I listen to alternative music mostly. My favorites are most definitely Paramore, Blue October, and Nine Inch Nails."

He grinned really big.

"That doesn't surprise me any. I had you figured for being a rocker. You have the whole Halsey thing going on."

I sank down in my seat. Little did he know I'd once had the whole Billie Eilish thing going on with my hair and the new look was definitely not on purpose. I turned my head to look out the window and didn't say anything. My long hair was just one of the many things taken from me because of my mother.

Landon turned onto a dirt road and pulled over to the side. He reached over and turned my chin toward him.

"Have I offended you? I didn't mean to. I really like the way you look," he said.

I could feel my eyes watering up, and before I knew what was happening, I was spilling it.

"My look a few months ago was more G.I. Jane; I'm sure you wouldn't have thought that looked good."

He grinned again.

"Jane, I'm pretty sure you would look good bald."

He looked me in the eye and ran the back of his hand down my cheek.

"This is a beautiful face, and I don't think it would matter what kind of hairstyle you have. You would still be beautiful."

When Landon touched my cheek, I got this weird shock in my stomach again. It didn't hurt; it actually felt kind of nice. What was up with that? He was still looking me right in the eye. His brown eyes made me want to be wrapped in his arms and stay there forever. There was something about him that made me feel very safe. That really scared me.

Landon turned his hand around so he was cupping my cheek.

"So, how did you end up with G.I. Jane hair anyway? That just doesn't seem like something any girl would do on purpose. But then again, we've already established you're not just any girl."

I broke his stare and looked out toward the window. Earlier that week, I'd sworn to myself I wouldn't expose any of my past to Landon or Milah Jo, and there I was letting Landon into my world already. What was wrong with me? I had more self-control than that.

"Let's just say this girl in my last foster home didn't like me much," I answered.

"Oh, Jane, I'm sorry. Was it very long before she got a hold of it?"

I frowned. I really missed my long hair.

"Yes, it was three-quarters down my back. Okay. That's all you get about me today. You'd better drive or we're going to be late."

Landon put his hand back on the steering wheel, put the car in gear, and pulled back out onto the road. He didn't pry any further, and I didn't reveal any more information.

I looked at the clock and realized it was already 10:30.

"How long will it take us to get there?" I asked. "I don't want Milah Jo to get worried."

The truth was I didn't want to give Landon any more time to get any more info out of me.

He glanced my way.

"We should be there in about ten more minutes. It's not far. We play in the woods behind my uncle's farm. He lives right outside of Sardinia."

It was quiet for a few minutes and I could hear some of the words of the country song that was playing. The words seemed familiar to me, so I reached over and turned the stereo up a little.

"Landon, I know this song."

He turned the stereo up some more and it was blaring Nine Inch Nails' "Hurt." But it wasn't Nine Inch Nails singing it; it was someone else.

"What the crap? Who is singing this song? This is a Nine Inch Nails song, not a country song," I blurted out.

Landon started laughing at me yet again.

"This is Johnny Cash," Landon said, "and he wore all black long before your Nine Inch Nails did. And according to you, he must have pretty good musical taste if he decided to cover a song you like. Maybe we country folk aren't so bad after all."

I had to admit I was a little embarrassed. I'd given Landon such a hard time about his music, and here I was enjoying a country version of one of my favorite songs.

"I'm sorry," I said. "I really need to quit making judgments about things I know nothing about."

Landon grinned.

"Yes, you do."

I'd definitely been put in my place a bit. I knew Landon had to have loved that.

Milah Jo was standing outside Kyle's car when we arrived at Landon's uncle's farm. She was grinning ear to ear. She must have enjoyed the ride. She was so easy to read. Everything she felt was always written all over her face.

Landon's uncle's farm was quite large. It had several barns and a huge house. This house wasn't like Landon's, though. It looked like it was falling apart. The paint on the wood siding was flaking off, some of the windows were cracked, and there was a giant hole in the flooring of the front porch. There were three older cars parked beside the house. Landon told me that his uncle, his uncle's girlfriend, and the girlfriend's younger sister lived there. He filled me in that it was his uncle on his mother's side and Landon wasn't really supposed to visit him. Landon said his uncle was kind of the black sheep of the family. He didn't go into detail why; he just said he wasn't going to be judgmental and stay away like the rest of his family did.

Landon parked the car, got the paintball equipment out of the trunk, and started walking toward Kyle and Milah Jo. He stopped halfway to Kyle's car and looked back at me with the strangest look. I guess that was my cue to get out of the car. I had to admit, I was a little nervous, but I got out and headed toward the others.

Landon and Kyle gave us the lowdown on the rules of a paintball war. There really weren't very many rules to it after all. It was pretty much "Don't get shot" and "Leave your facemask on at all times." The guys flipped a coin and determined that Landon and I would go out to get settled in the woods and then Kyle and Milah Jo would follow shortly to hunt us. We fired a couple of practice shots, put on our camouflage gear, and were on our way. Thank goodness the guys hadn't decided to gang up against Milah Jo and me. We wouldn't have stood a chance.

Landon and I walked a long time into the woods before he decided on a good spot for us to hide. He'd found a pile of brush just behind a pond. He said the brush would be good cover for us and the openness around the pond would give us plenty of time to see our hunters coming. This was starting to sound scarier by the minute. Landon was starting to sound like the people in military documentaries. It was definitely too late to turn back.

So there I lay in the woods with all the spiders and creepy crawlers that lived there. It was a gross feeling to know that, at any time, something could crawl into my pant leg. The thought of it made me shiver. Landon must have sensed I was getting uncomfortable because he scooted closer to me. We had to be quiet because we didn't want Kyle and Milah Jo to find us. The idea was for us to see them first and get a good shot on them before they found us. The good thing about being quiet was that Landon couldn't question me anymore about my past. The bad thing was that the silence gave me plenty of time to think about all the stuff that was living in those half-wet leaves beneath me.

After lying in the leaves and brush for about ten minutes, we finally heard something coming. The sound wasn't coming from the area we'd come from; it was coming from behind us. I was a little scared—how would Kyle and Milah Jo have gotten in behind us like that? Landon looked at me and pointed at my paintball gun. Then he grabbed my facemask and pulled it down over my face. I was so nervous that my heavy breathing fogged up the damn thing and I couldn't see anything. I turned around to try to figure out what was going on when I thought I heard shots. I didn't know what to do. I couldn't see and I didn't know where to go. I pulled up my paintball gun and just started randomly firing. After what seemed like about fifty rounds, I heard someone yelling. It was Landon. I pulled up my facemask because I couldn't hear or see with the damn thing on. As I was pulling up the mask, I heard a shot fired. It was too late; my mask was already off and the paintball hit me right below my left eye. It hurt like hell. I grabbed my eye. I tried to keep my cool, but I couldn't do it. I fell to the ground while still holding my eye.

Landon came over and knelt down beside me.

"Jane, are you okay?"

I looked up with the only eye I could see out of and saw that Landon's jacket was peppered with pink paintball splatters. I was the only one with pink paintballs.

"Did I shoot you?"

Landon chuckled and said, "Yeah, you totally went postal on me, City Girl. Let me see your eye. Are you okay? I'm so sorry. I should have had you put that mask on sooner so it wouldn't have fogged up so bad on you during all the action."

I took my hand down from my eye, and the look on Landon's face told me it wasn't a pretty sight. It was throbbing now. Milah Jo came running over to me. She was hysterically apologizing. I couldn't figure out why she was so upset until I looked down and saw the purple paint on my hand. She was the one who'd shot me in the eye.

I looked up at her and asked what had happened.

"Kyle over there made me run all the way around the woods so we could come in behind you guys," Milah Jo said, frowning. "He said it was a surefire way we would win. When we were getting close, we heard shots."

She pointed at Kyle and said, "Genius here said you were firin' on us and told me to shoot back. I'm so sorry, Jane. I didn't know ya didn't have your mask on. Look at your face. I'm so sorry."

Kyle was standing over by a huge tree laughing.

"We told you girls never to take your masks off," he said. "You should have listened. Ain't no amount of makeup going to cover that shiner up."

Milah Jo flipped him off.

"Shut up, freak," she said. "Can't you see she's hurt?"

Wow! He'd really done something to piss her off in the short time we'd been apart. She wasn't gushing over him at all anymore.

Landon shot Kyle a dirty look.

"Come on, Jane, let me help you up," Landon said. "We need to get some ice on that eye."

As I stood up, I got another look at his pink-splattered jacket.

"Landon, I'm so sorry," I said. "I had no idea I was shooting you. I couldn't see. Are you all right?"

Landon put his arm around me to help me walk to the car.

"It's my fault, Jane. I should have told you to put the mask on when we got settled by the brush pile. I was so busy admiring your pretty face that I didn't want you to cover it up. It was very selfish of me, and for that I'm sorry."

It made me nervous to hear him talk about me like that. So instead of thanking him for the compliment, I started stomping through the woods back toward the car.

"I can tell you one thing, Landon Whitman," I said. "I don't want to play paintball with you anymore."

I smiled at him to let him know I was okay. He returned the smile.

"That's quite all right, Jane Michaels, because I believe I have a few bruises that tell me I don't want to play paintball with you anymore either."

We both started laughing. I didn't laugh long, though, because it sure did hurt my eye to move any muscle in my face.

Milah Jo decided to catch a ride back with Landon and me. Evidently Kyle wasn't all she thought he would be. Kyle didn't seem too heartbroken. He'd decided to hang out at Landon's uncle's house. I would say he'd only agreed to pick up Milah Jo and play today as a favor to Landon anyway.

We weren't on the road for five minutes when Milah Jo chimed in with her cheery voice.

"So, guys, since this bombed, I think we should have a do-over. What do you all want to do tonight?"

Landon smiled at her in the rear-view mirror.

"Milah Jo, it took some convincing to get Jane to do this with us today," he said. "Do you think we could get her out of the house twice in one day?"

I smiled out the window. On my eye, I was holding the make-shift ice pack Landon had made for me. I loved it when people talked about you as if you weren't there.

"You know I'm sitting right here, guys. Maybe you should ask Jane?"

Landon started laughing.

"There's a party out at the old Newman houses tonight if you girls would want to go," he said.

The idea of doing something that night sounded cool, but I didn't know if I would be up for going to a party where a bunch of his friends would be.

"I'm not real big on social events," I said. "I don't know about that one. I'm not exactly a favorite among your friends, remember?"

Milah Jo came out of her seat belt and plopped her head in between the two front seats.

"Come on, Jane, it'll be fun. Me and Landon will be by your side the whole time."

I frowned. "I don't know if Mother is going to let me back out of the house after she sees this shiner."

"Well, come to my house then," Milah Jo said. "You can get ready there. Then you won't have to explain it to her until tomorrow, hon. You're so tiny. I bet my little sister has something you can wear."

Landon put his hand on my leg.

"Sounds good to me," he said. "Do you want to?"

Oh my gosh—he was doing it again. He made me so freaking nervous! I let out a heavy sigh and agreed to go to the party.

Great—I was going to a party. There were going to be a bunch of people there I didn't even like and I was going to have to prance around with this huge shiner. Nice.

"I guess so," I said. "What are you people doing to me? Believe it or not, I used to be pretty good at saying no."

Great! It's party time

Landon dropped us off at Milah Jo's house, and I called Mother to ask her if I could spend the night. Mother was so happy I was staying with a friend that she didn't even ask about our paintball adventure. Milah Jo's grandparents' house was old but very cozy. It was warm and inviting. The house was clean, but you could definitely tell a lot of people lived there. Seven people lived in that three-bedroom house. Milah Jo and her sister shared a bedroom with their mom. That probably would have been pretty awkward in any other family, but not this one. The three of them had late-night discussions in their room almost every night. I think Milah Jo's mom was more of a friend than a mother. Milah Jo was allowed to do pretty much whatever she wanted.

Milah Jo's Maw and Paw seemed really nice. When we arrived, Maw was in the kitchen cooking something that smelled very good and Paw was in the barn working on an old tractor. Milah Jo made sure she took me out there to meet him. He was friendly but was totally focused on what he was working on. Milah Jo's sister was two years younger than Milah Jo. She was built somewhat like me, but would she have anything I would be comfortable wearing? She dressed a little more revealing than I did. I couldn't very well go to a party in my muddy, leaf-covered clothes, though.

Milah Jo also had two younger brothers who were maybe eight and ten. They were cute, but I couldn't understand a word those boys said. They had quite the Southern drawl!

Of course, everyone asked me about my eye. Milah Jo just giggled and told everyone she was a much better shot than she'd imagined she would be. Seemed she wasn't feeling too bad about it anymore. I didn't think it was very funny, considering my eye was still throbbing and she hadn't even been aiming at me. Milah Jo's Maw offered me a piece of steak to put on my eye. I tried to be very considerate when I declined.

The day went pretty quickly at Milah Jo's. It took us forever to figure out what we were going to wear to the party. Milah Jo finally decided what I was wearing and told me I had no choice and to suck it up. The outfit was a little bolder than anything I would normally wear. Thank goodness I had my jacket to hide beneath. Milah Jo's Maw fed us one of the best suppers I'd ever had in my life. I savored every minute of it until I found out I'd been eating Bambi's poor mother. How awful! I'm not a vegetarian, but for some reason I'd always had a real problem with eating a deer. A pig or a cow I could eat; they're fat and sloppy. They were definitely created to be eaten. A deer, on the other hand, is dainty and graceful. They have a beauty about them and I just couldn't bring myself to intentionally eat one. It didn't help that, where I came from, not too many people ate deer. But when you got out into the country, they lived on deer. I made sure to let Milah Jo know to warn me next time so I wouldn't eat the poor little things.

Landon was ten minutes late picking us up. I was feeling a little relieved thinking I wouldn't have to go to that party until I started thinking that maybe Landon had changed his mind about me. I was sure he'd skipped out on us until he pulled into the driveway. He apologized for being late and told us he'd had to drop his sister off at the car dealership to pick up her new SUV.

The party was hopping. There were people everywhere. It was pretty dark, so people really didn't notice my black eye, which was definitely a plus. No one at the party went out of their way to talk to me, but at least no one was rude. We found a spot next to the bonfire, and I was glad to sit somewhere warm because I was freezing. Milah Jo decided to mingle, so that left me and Landon there alone. There were other people sitting by the fire, but they were scattered all around.

It was a pretty good night. Landon asked me all kinds of questions about my life before I'd come to Winchester. He already knew I'd been in foster care, so I told him a few things about being in foster care and being away from Lizzie. But I never told him why I'd been in foster care, just that Mother had made some mistakes. He asked me about my father and why I hadn't just lived with him. I explained to him that I'd never met my father and that I didn't even know his name. It sounded like such a sad story, and I couldn't believe I was spilling it all to him. He put his arm around me and told me he was sorry I'd had to go through all that. Despite the fact that I'd sworn I wouldn't put myself out there like that, there I was telling Landon things about my life that I didn't want anyone to know.

We stayed at the party until about midnight. Milah Jo had been quite the social butterfly, and it took us forever to find her so we could head out of there. While we were looking for her, we ran into two guys I'd never seen before. They didn't seem very friendly and they told Landon they would be sure to catch up with him later. Landon didn't seem too concerned about them and I didn't ask any questions.

I had to admit I'd had a pretty good time. Landon was so easy to talk to, and he seemed to hang on my every word. He looked me straight in the eye when he talked to me or when I was talking to him. I had the hardest time looking at him when he looked at me so intently like that. He was so different from me. I realized I was completely falling for him. He was gorgeous, no doubt, but there really was so much more to him that I never would have known had I not given in to him. To sit and talk with him, you would never have guessed he was loaded. He seemed so humble.

When we got back to Milah Jo's house, Landon shut the car off and asked her if it was okay if he kept me for the rest of the night. He wanted to know if her mom would call my mother and get me in trouble. Milah Jo assured him her mom wouldn't do that. They almost looked as if they'd already planned this part of the night and their conversation was just for my benefit. I just kept looking at Landon strangely, and he finally asked me if I minded to spend the night with him instead of going with Milah Jo. I made sure to ask him what it was he had in mind for the rest of the night. I told him outright that I was not one of those easy girls who would sleep with a guy on the first date. He assured me that was not his intention and that he would be a perfect gentleman. He also reminded me that I had insisted over and over that this was not a date, so it didn't matter. I knew better than to agree to it, but once again I couldn't help myself. I really did want to spend more time with him. So, I agreed.

I wasn't sure what to expect. We drove for a little while just talking. He kept looking over at me. I didn't know why he kept doing that. What in the world did he see in me? I was a lot of things, but special I was not. After about an hour of driving around, we ended up on a bumpy little gravel road. My *Wrong Turn* fears once again kicked in. I never should have watched that movie; I didn't like scary movies anyway. I thought I knew better.

Now, any off-road, wooded area was going to scare the crap right out of me. The road ended and Landon put the car in park.

I frowned at him.

"Landon Whitman, I told you I am not one of those girls," I said. "You can take me back to Milah Jo's house now."

He smiled that amazing smile at me.

"Well, Jane Michaels, just maybe I'm not that kind of guy. There's an awesome wooded area up the trail just a little. We call it the pines. There are so many pine trees, the ground is completely covered with pine needles. There's a pond that's right up against it. It's beautiful. The moon is full tonight so I figured we'd be able to see it pretty well. I thought I would show you something you could appreciate and prove to you it's not just cow country out here, City Girl."

I couldn't help but smile at him. I had to admit I liked it when he called me "City Girl."

"It sounds really nice, but don't you think it's kind of cold out?" I countered. "I'm sure you can't start a fire in the middle of all those pine needles."

Of course he smiled at me again.

"Well, we could if we wanted to start a massive forest fire," he said. "I have some blankets in the boot of the car. We can use those to sit on, but this is one of those rare nights when the temperature goes up. It's already ten degrees warmer than what it was when we were at the party."

He pointed up at the thermometer.

"See, it's sixty degrees outside. That's not cold."

I never watched the news; I'd had no idea it was supposed to get warmer. I'd thought it always got colder at night. We gathered the stuff out of the car and headed toward the pine trees. I could see them now. Landon spread out the blanket, sat down, and patted the spot next to him. I sat down and looked out over the pond. The moonlight was beautiful reflecting off the pond. I'd never seen anything like it before. The smell of the night air and the pine trees was so crisp and refreshing. The pine needles actually made a pretty good cushion to sit on and the pine trees felt like they offered protection from the rest of the world. I'd never felt as much peace as I did sitting there next to Landon in the midst of all that beauty and protection. It was amazing.

In that moment, I felt that Landon really did understand me. We talked through the night, and he really was the perfect gentleman. He never once tried to kiss me. It seemed as if the night hadn't lasted long enough before it was time to leave. We'd been together for almost twenty-four hours, yet it didn't seem like it had been nearly enough. Yep, I was definitely falling for this boy. How had this happened? I could have sworn I'd had my guard up the whole time.

More stormy weather

Landon dropped me off at Milah Jo's a little after seven on Sunday morning, and Milah Jo's grandpa took me home around eight. Milah Jo was still sleeping, so I just left her a note to call me later. I ate breakfast with Lizzie and ignored Mother, then headed off to bed. I needed some sleep. I didn't get it, though. Every time I would drift off, I would dream of how Landon was going to break my heart or how Mother was going to screw up everything and I would have to leave Landon. It was my subconscious telling me I should get off this road I was going down before it was too late. I decided that as much as I liked Landon, I couldn't take the risk. I had to end it before it even really got started. That was the only way. It had to be done and it had to be soon.

I decided I would just ignore Landon until he realized there was nothing between us. He sat with Milah Jo and me at lunch and I didn't even acknowledge he was there. It was so hard. Milah Jo kept asking me why I was being so rude to him. I just told her I didn't want to be involved with anyone. Landon quit sitting with us after a few days. It was awful. As much as it had irritated me that he wouldn't get the hint those first few days, it hurt that he'd given up. I felt like such a nut job. I knew I couldn't have it both ways. Milah Jo didn't give up, though. She had something to say every day about how I must have been insane to push Landon away like that.

After two weeks of me ignoring Landon, he caught up with me when I got off the bus at the end of the lane. I kept walking toward the house, but he stayed right next to me the whole way, asking me what was wrong and telling me how he'd thought we'd really hit it off and that he couldn't understand why I was being so rude to him again. I finally just stopped and yelled at him that there was nothing there, there never would be, and the other night had been a mistake. He looked at me so strangely. I thought it might have been one of the most heartbreaking looks I'd ever seen. Why would he care that I didn't want anything to do with him? He hadn't known me that long. What was the big deal? I took off walking to the house and he just stood there. I didn't know what he was doing because I never looked back to find out. I couldn't.

Milah Jo had talked me into going to some kind of carnival that was going on in Winchester. I didn't want to go, but she wouldn't leave it alone. She said she'd heard that a really good local rock band, Rootbound, was playing and she thought we should go. She insisted we go early, though, so we could walk around and get something to eat.

It was the smallest carnival I'd ever seen. There were more people selling stuff out of their yards than there were fair booths. I saw Mrs. Whitman sitting at one of the local church booths. She spotted me and motioned for me to come over. She was sitting with two other ladies who looked to be just as prominent as she was. I couldn't be rude to Mother's boss, so I went over to her. She introduced me to the other women as her housemaid's daughter and made sure to give me a pamphlet about the free store the church had. She told me I might be able to find some nicer clothes and some decent shoes there. She definitely didn't like me or the way I dressed, but I didn't understand why a grown woman would get her kicks out of picking on a teenager. She must have, though, because she'd just humiliated me in front of everyone around the booth. It was a good thing I'd decided not to have anything to do with Landon. Mrs. Whitman really would have liked that, I'm sure. I just set the pamphlet down and walked away. As we left, Milah Jo was banging her lips the whole time about how rude "that woman" had been. I then informed her it was Landon's mother, and she couldn't believe it. She said there was no way Landon had come from that woman. I just nodded and agreed.

We ate and headed to the area where the concert was supposed to be. It was really crowded, and there was no way we were going to find good seats. It looked like it was standing room only. That was when Milah Jo let me know someone was saving seats for us in the front. I couldn't figure out who she would have talked into that. I followed her up the aisle and saw Landon sitting front and center. Suddenly I realized they'd planned this together.

Milah Jo hurried herself into the end seat so I would be sandwiched between her and Landon. He looked over at me when I sat down and gave me that one-in-a-million, smug smile of his. I knew right then that I was going to have to leave. I wouldn't be able to resist him while being that close to him. I turned to Milah Jo and told her I was going to find a ride home. I got up and started pushing my way through the crowd. Once I'd made it past the hair salon on the corner, I realized I didn't really know anyone who could give me a ride home. I shrugged my shoulders and decided I would just walk home.

I'd made it out past the railroad tracks when I felt something wet plop down on my arm, then again on my nose. I looked up at the sky and realized it looked angry. How had I not noticed the weather until then? I'd been outside for a few hours and hadn't seen the dark clouds headed our way. It didn't take long for the rain to start coming down in buckets. I was absolutely drenched, but I just kept walking forward. I should have known something would happen. Something *always* happens. I was starting to get really cold and felt like I had an inch of water in my shoes when I heard that familiar engine roar. I turned to look, and sure enough it was Landon.

He pulled up beside me and smiled that smile.

"You look like you might need a ride," he gloated.

I looked at him and said sarcastically, "Oh, yeah? Well, I don't. So you just go on down the road, Mustang Boy. I'll be fine."

He shook his head.

"You may be fine now, but it's starting to lightning and it's just crazy to be out walking in this kind of weather. Come on, Jane, my interior is getting wet. Get in."

I started walking faster.

"Then put up your damn window, Landon," I shot back. "Don't let that pretty little car get messed up on my account."

Landon pulled the car to the side of the road, got out, and caught up to me.

"What the hell is your problem, Jane? Get in the car before you get yourself hurt," he yelled.

I didn't say anything. I just kept walking. I knew if I got in that car with him, there would be no way I could defy him. I wanted to be with him so much. I hadn't realized it would be so hard to push him away. I hadn't known him that long, but it was like there was this weird connection to him that was so strong and I couldn't help but want him.

Landon ran up in front of me, stopped, and blocked me from going any farther.

"Jane, please get into the car. It's getting really bad out here. It's dangerous."

I crossed my arms and stood there. He was making me so mad. Why couldn't he just make this easy for me?

"Go away, Landon."

He threw his hands in the air.

"I can't, Jane. Don't you understand that? All I want anymore is to spend every minute of my time with you. Do you think I enjoy this? I never had this problem before you came along. I couldn't have cared less about anybody but myself. Now you're all I ever think about. My world is spinning completely out of control without you in it."

Before I could respond to what Landon had said, golf-ball-sized hail started falling from the sky. That stuff hurt! And just like that, Landon picked me up and threw me over his shoulder.

"You're going to get in that damn car before we both get knocked out!" he yelled.

He opened the car door and put me in the passenger seat. He was furious when he climbed into the driver's seat, and he was quiet for what seemed like an eternity. I assumed he was calming himself down before he spoke again. He turned the heat up on high and the rush of warm air felt wonderful, because I was freezing. He reached into the back seat and grabbed a hooded sweatshirt.

"Here, put this on before you freeze to death or catch pneumonia," he advised.

I grabbed the sweatshirt and went to put it on over my wet clothes. He snatched it out of my hands.

"It's not going to do you any good if you keep your wet clothes on, goof."

"Well, I'm not going to change in front of you, moron!" I snapped back.

Landon stifled a laugh.

"I won't watch. I'll turn my head, I promise. Here, you might as well put these on too."

He handed me a pair of his sweatpants and I wondered why he kept all these clothes in the back of his car anyway. He turned to the window and started changing into a different T-shirt. I just sat there and stared at him while he changed his shirt. He looked amazing. I was so glad he hadn't caught me staring at him after I'd just yelled at him not to look at me. As nervous as it made me, I went ahead and changed my clothes. I was freezing, and I couldn't stand to be cold. I did leave on my wet bra and underwear, though. There was no way I was completely stripping down in front of Landon.

The hail had stopped, but the rain was still coming down really hard, so Landon decided we'd better just sit still until the rain let up. Boy, that had worked out well for him! I was trapped. There was no way I was going back out in that crap since I was dry and getting warm. But the silence was getting to me. It gave me too much time to think about him. I had a hard enough time blocking out Landon when I wasn't near him; to be in the car with him was driving me crazy. His scent filled the car. His hair was soaked and dripping. I couldn't stop looking at him. His dry T-shirt formed around his wet chest and arms, and he looked absolutely gorgeous. That time he caught me staring at him, but I didn't look away. I held his eyes in mine and knew in that moment that I was already too far gone. There was no turning back.

I felt a tear run down my cheek. Landon reached over and wiped it away.

"Why are you crying?"

I let out a sigh.

"Because I'm an idiot. I should have gotten in the car with you when you told me to, I shouldn't have ignored you for the past few weeks, and I should have listened to my gut and just gone for it. You scare the crap right out of me, Landon Whitman."

He grabbed my hands and held them in his.

"I don't understand why, Jane. Am I so bad that you're afraid to be with me? What did I do that would make you afraid of me?"

I pulled my hands away from his.

"You didn't do anything, Landon. It's me, not you. I can't take the chance of getting close to someone and having them taken away from me. I've been there too many times with Mother and Lizzie, and I don't want to do it again. Especially not with you. I don't think I could survive losing you now."

The rain had started to ease up.

Landon looked at me for a few minutes and then turned away to begin the drive toward home. He smiled and mumbled something about "the old 'It's me, not you'" line. Thank goodness the ride home was pretty quiet. I'd said enough already.

At home, Landon pulled the car into the garage and I got out quickly. I didn't want to say anymore. He caught me as I walked around the car. He put his arms around me and held me tight.

"Don't fight this, Jane," he said. "I won't hurt you."

Landon pulled away just enough so his face was in front of mine. I melted; I just gave in. I would just have to be ready to deal with whatever would come my way. I couldn't deny it anymore: I needed him.

I looked Landon in the eyes and admitted it.

"As much as I've fought it, I can't anymore. You win."

He looked back at me with those brown eyes that made me feel like he could see right into my soul and whispered in my ear, "I don't know what took you so long. I feel like I've been waiting for you all my life. I don't know how I ever lived without you."

I interrupted him. If I heard anymore, I might never be able to go back to who I'd been before I met him.

"I'm so scared, Landon. My life is different from yours. I may get yanked out of my mother's house tomorrow and end up in a foster home four hours away. What then? I already care too much for you. If I get in any deeper, I don't think I could make it through our separation."

He put his hands around my waist, lifted me up onto the hood of his Mustang, and moved closer to me until my legs were straddled around his waist. I was pretty sure my face was getting red and my heart was skipping beats. I'd never been that intimate with anyone.

Landon smiled at me.

"Jane, I don't think you understand how deep you are already in. If you leave me now, I'll follow you to the ends of the earth. Why can't you allow yourself just a little happiness? Allow me to love you the way you deserve to be loved. You've put a wall around yourself refusing to let anyone near it, let alone in it. I understand that you've been hurt, but I won't give up. I won't stop until you love me back. I want to make you smile every day for the rest of your life."

He kissed my forehead, then lifted me down from the car.

I looked him straight in the eye.

"Landon, I lost my smile long ago. If you could return it to me, that would be greatly appreciated."

He chuckled and replied, "That will become my life's mission, Miss Jane: to return you your smile."

"That sounds good to me," I agreed.

I heard a car coming down the driveway and glanced out the window to see it was Mrs. Whitman. I told Landon I was not ready to deal with his mother finding out about us, especially since I was wearing Landon's clothes. He said he really didn't care what she thought. I told him I had to go, kissed him on the cheek, and bolted for the door.

I went out the back door of the garage and into the back door of our little house. Mother and Lizzie were out, so I had the house to myself. I went into the bedroom, lay down, and went over in my head the conversation I'd just had with Landon. *How could I have let that happen?* When I'd first moved here, I'd thought he was a self-centered, arrogant ass. Wasn't that my first impression of him? I got so upset when I felt like people had judged me before they knew me, yet that is exactly what I'd done to Landon. How had everything changed so much in eight short weeks?

Things would never be the same. He was tearing down my wall. I was so afraid that if he got it down, I might fall to pieces. Yet, I was more afraid that if I didn't let him in, I might regret it forever. All I knew was I didn't want to lose the feeling I had at that very moment. I could still feel his warmth on my lips, smell his scent on the clothes I was wearing, and feel that crazy, electricity in the pit of my stomach.

Confessions

Mother had been driving me nuts. She was still trying to have a relationship with me. I didn't know why she wouldn't just leave me alone and get on with her life. She was spending at least three nights a week with her NA buddies by that point. I enjoyed the alone time with Lizzie, but I often wondered what Mother was up to when she was gone. She seemed to be keeping it straight when she was home. *She'd better not screw this up*, I thought.

Mother had forced me to go to the grocery store with her and Lizzie the day before. It was such a joke. I knew we were getting food stamps. I really didn't want to go to the store with her while she spent them, but since they were putting them on that card now, I thought nobody would be able to tell we were using them. Wrong. We went to the local grocery store—the smallest grocery store I'd ever been in. There was a horse and buggy parked in a grassy area next to the store. I still wasn't used to seeing Amish people around. I do believe they stared at me in the store more than I stared at them. I heard the woman talking to one of the teenage girls in a different language. I figured she was probably telling her I was some kind of abomination.

It was a great boost to my ego to be talked about even if I didn't know what they were saying. I really thought I looked pretty normal. I didn't understand why people looked at me so strangely just because I had a few extra piercings. They must not have gotten out of the sticks much. People in the city were much more eccentric than I am. I didn't stand out at all there. I was so glad Milah Jo wasn't with me; she would have gone off on the family for staring. That girl had no filter, whereas I wasn't that outspoken.

The worst part of the grocery store trip came at the checkout lane. I was loading stuff onto the counter and didn't realize that Emily's sidekick, Maria, was in line behind us. It made me a little nervous at first until I realized that if Mother concealed the food card well enough, Maria wouldn't see it. I relaxed and moved up to the end of the counter. I looked over at Mother when she was paying for the groceries. That's when I saw the words "Food Stamp Purchase" on the huge computer screen above the register. Maria saw it too, then turned and gave me the most sarcastic smile. She didn't say anything then, but I was sure she was saving it for later. She wouldn't keep that kind of ammo to herself.

I didn't say a word all the way home. Mother should have never made me go with them. It was all her fault.

• • • • •

Ohio has always had the craziest weather, no matter what part of the state you're in. It can be snowing one day and beach weather the next. On this day, it was eighty-two degrees. I didn't want to stay in the house all day with Mother, so I decided to take a walk. I hadn't talked to Landon since I'd left him in the garage. I really wanted to see him, but I wasn't about to go to the Whitmans' looking for him. I didn't want to deal with his mother or his sister. I hadn't been in the garage, so I didn't know if he was even home. I decided I would walk out past the barn and check out this pond Lizzie had been talking about. Mother had walked her out there a few weeks ago to show her it was very deep and dangerous. Mother had also assured her that there were no jellyfish in it.

Lizzie was still determined that she was going to go jellyfishing in that pond. That scared me. I didn't want Lizzie to go out there and fall in. I couldn't swim and I wouldn't have been able to save her. I sure would try, though.

I found a good sunny spot to sit down and relax. I loved the feeling of the sun beating down on my face. I just loved being warm. There was something about the sun's rays, almost as if you could drink them in. Nothing could recharge me more than the sun. I loved it. I was leaning back with my eyes closed enjoying the sunshine so I didn't hear Landon when he snuck up on me. I jumped; he'd scared the crap out of me. He just laughed and sat down next to me.

I rose up and folded my arms.

"What are you doing out here? Are you stalking me?" I snapped.

He held out his fishing pole and his tackle box.

"I didn't know you were out here," he said. "I decided that since it's such a nice day, I would go fishing. Everything isn't always about you, Jane, although it's a nice surprise to find you here."

He smiled that crazy beautiful smile.

"Oh, sorry. I tend to be a little sarcastic sometimes. It's a defense mechanism. It's hard to turn off," I admitted.

"Yeah, I think we're going to have to work on that," Landon replied. "I can't have you biting my head off every time we're together. So do you want to sit at the dock with me while I reel in a big one?"

"I should have known a farm boy like you would know how to fish. Lizzie has been driving me and Mother crazy about bringing her out here to go fishing. I keep trying to explain to her that I have no idea how it's done," I said.

"Well, maybe I could take the two of you fishing soon," he offered.

I laughed at Landon and he looked at me in disappointment. I didn't mean to, but I thought I might have hurt his feelings. I put my hand on his shoulder.

"That would be great," I said, "but she's expecting to catch some jellyfish, so I'm sure she'd end up getting mad. We've been trying to explain to her that jellyfish are only in the ocean, but she just ends up getting frustrated with us. She's only four. She has no idea how to control that temper of hers yet."

Landon smiled again.

"Let me guess: She likes SpongeBob? She also sounds like she's a lot like her sister. From what I've seen, her sister doesn't know how to control her temper yet either."

"I do too!" I snapped. "And yes, she loves SpongeBob."

Landon kept smiling. He enjoyed pushing my buttons.

"Believe it or not," he told me, "there's a lake not too far from here that has freshwater jellyfish around August or September every year. We could take her if you want."

He was talking about taking me somewhere in August or September. It was only May. I didn't know about this. What if Mother screwed up and I wasn't living here in August or September? It really excited me to know he was planning on being with me a few months from now.

I told Landon that Lizzie would enjoy that and we would go as long as Lizzie and I still lived there then. He didn't understand that we were a transient family. I should have been born a gypsy. I never got to stay in one place very long. I couldn't believe I'd given in. I'd had the distance thing down pat until I met Landon, but I definitely had fallen for that boy. There was no fighting it anymore. I was drawn to him.

We ended up sitting on the dock for hours talking. I don't think he ever ended up casting his pole into the water. He was so easy to talk to. I told him about all kinds of things I normally would not have told anyone. I told him about all the awful foster homes I'd lived in over the past few years. I didn't dare tell him about Mother, though. He didn't know why I'd been in foster care, and I didn't plan on telling him any time soon. It was pretty crazy that I would tell him I was the bastard child of some nameless man but I was too embarrassed to tell him my mother loved drugs more than she loved me.

I had a hard time sleeping that night. All I could think about was the wonderful day I'd had with Landon. If I went to sleep, then I would have to wake up to the reality that it was back to school and back to being treated like a leper. Thank goodness there were only a few weeks of school left. Then I wouldn't have to deal with all the hate drama.

The first thing I saw when I got to school Monday was my locker covered with words written in permanent marker: "Spawn of a heroin-addicted welfare whore." I should have known something was coming. They usually put the slander up on posters, but this time it was more lasting. There was no taking that down, and it wasn't going to just wash off either. I was trying to figure out a way to deal with it when I saw Milah Jo coming at me looking mad as hell.

"I already saw my locker, Milah Jo," I told her. "Calm down, okay?"

She gave me that "I don't give a hoot" look and hissed, "Do you know what I heard Emily telling folks today? She was talking about you and said your mom is a heroin addict and that her mom took y'all in as a charity case. How can she justify going around telling lies like that? It's absolutely ridiculous. She's such a bitch."

My whole world went spinning out of control. I'd managed to keep hidden the fact that my mother was a heroin addict. I hadn't even told Landon. How had Emily found out? I knew she was pissed about me and Landon dating, but I didn't think she disliked me this much. What would Landon think of me when he found out? I grabbed Milah Jo's arm and dragged her down the hall and out the side door.

"Milah Jo," I began, "she isn't lying about my mother. She *is* a heroin addict. As for the charity part, my mother works for Mrs. Whitman. She earns our keep."

Milah Jo gave me this weird look and said, "Wow, you're kidding me, right? I knew you had a grudge against your mom, but I wasn't sure why. I just thought Emily was making up lies about you, hon. I would have never believed it. Your mom seems so normal. It doesn't matter if it's the truth or a lie; it sure doesn't change the way I feel about you or the fact that what they did was wrong!"

I decided it was time to tell Milah Jo the truth. She'd been a good friend to me after all.

"I know Mother puts on a good show, but she's not what she seems," I explained. "She claims to be clean for the past six months, but I'm not so sure. She's been hanging out a lot with these so-called friends she met at her NA meetings. They don't even go to the NA meetings anymore. She says they have their own meetings because they understand each other so much more than the other people who went to the meetings. I asked her why she just didn't go to a different NA meeting. She said since we live so far out in the country, there's only one NA meeting within thirty miles. That's crazy. There are meetings everywhere in the city."

"Maybe she *is* having meetings with them," Milah Jo suggested.

"Yeah, I know my mom. She's lying through her teeth. She wouldn't know the truth if it jumped up and bit her right in the ass. It's just a matter of time before she does something that draws the attention of Children Services, and then that's it. They come and take me and Lizzie away and I lose everything all over again. I lose Lizzie, I lose Landon, and I lose you. I swore I would not get close to anyone. You guys forced your way in, and now I'm going to lose you too."

Milah Jo put her arm around me and demanded, "Come on, Jane, don't be such a drama queen. You ain't gonna lose me. Me and you, we're tight. We'll always be friends, no matter where you are. Haven't you heard of texting? Besides, you ain't goin' anywhere—I'll make sure of it. If I'm stuck here, you're gonna be stuck here with me."

I hugged Milah Jo.

"I'm so sorry, Milah Jo. I should have told you. You're my best friend and I should have trusted you. Trust is very hard for me, you know?"

"You don't even know that your mom is doin' that stuff again. So it won't even come to that, sugar," she assured me.

"Oh, yes I do. All the signs are there."

"And how do you know about all the signs? Girl, you're only fifteen years old. I'll tell ya what my mama always tells me: You may think ya know everything, but ya don't."

"Well, obviously I've been through it before. I also read every book on addiction I could get my hands on last time we were taken from home. I learned a lot between the two. I've discovered that addiction takes everything from you. If you're addicted to a drug, it will make you lose everything you have. But what the books don't tell you—this I learned from experience—is that you don't have to be addicted to a drug for it to take everything from you. All you have to do is love someone who's addicted to drugs. Because their drug use will take everything *you* have too. I'm living proof. It takes everything you love and everything that's important to you. It also takes your pride, your dignity, and your self-esteem. This person who is supposed to love you more than anything can't love you enough to stop doing the drugs. That makes you feel worthless. How can she love this drug more than me? I have no pride left. Look where I come from—why would I? Emily can tell the world anything she wants; I don't care as long as you and Landon don't judge me for it."

I started crying.

"Girl, do ya really think me or Landon would judge you?" Milah Jo asked. "Especially for something that's not your fault? You have no control over what your mom does, and when I get a hold of Miss Holier than Thou Emily Whitman, she's gonna wish she'd never opened her big, fat mouth. She's gonna get it Southern-style. Guaranteed! This is ridiculous. It has to stop. I wish I had something on her to make her squirm and put her panties in a bunch."

I wasn't sure how much abuse I was supposed to take before I lost my freaking mind. I could handle a lot, but geez, man, they would just not let up. Milah Jo was great. She always had my back, and the way she insisted she was going to get her chance to pounce on Emily cracked me up.

Of course, Landon had heard about everything. I couldn't bring myself to tell him that everything Emily had said was the truth, and he never asked if it was. He assured me at lunch that he would take care of things and it would not happen again. He was pretty sure his sister was behind the Jane bashing. Milah Jo was ready to just go take her out. She kept telling me to say the word and she would lay Emily out flat. I let her know I really appreciated her sticking up for me, but I didn't want to be involved in anything that would get me in trouble. I sure didn't want to do anything to draw the attention of Children Services. And as for Emily and Maria, I would not play into their drama. After all, it was just words. At least, that's what I kept telling myself.

Landon and I enjoyed the next month with no incidents. The Jane bashing and the graffiti on my locker did indeed stop, so there was no more drama at school. I refused to let Mother or Mrs. Whitman know we were dating, so there was no drama there either. Landon and I stole our moments together whenever we could. I couldn't believe Emily had not let the cat out of the bag to her mother. Whatever it was Landon said to her to make her back off must have worked, because she left us alone completely. He must have had some really good dirt on her.

I don't think I'd ever had so much fun in my life as I did in that month. By that time, school was out and we were starting to enjoy the summer. Landon took me to different places in the county to show me all the beauty of this home that he loved so much. He insisted I would love this place as much as he did by the time he was done and that I would never want to leave. He took me to a rock quarry where the water was beautiful, he made me hike to the top of a place called Buzzards Roost that was amazing, he took me to numerous covered bridges, he fed me at a wonderful restaurant nestled way out in the country called Murphin Ridge Inn, and he showed me the beauty of an Indian burial site called Serpent Mound.

I would have to say my favorite place in the small county was the pines. That was the first place we'd been alone together, and for that it was special. We spent a good bit of our time there. It was very private, which was good since our relationship was still a secret from our mothers. I knew we would not be able to keep up the charade much longer. Whenever we were out in public, Milah Jo was with us so it looked more like we were all hanging out together. She didn't seem to mind hanging out. She always said it gave her something to do.

Missing

The summer was shaping up to be one of the best times of my life. Landon and I were having a great time. I was even starting to tolerate Mother a little better.

It was a day in early July when Mother and Mrs. Whitman found out Landon and I were dating. Mother had gone to West Union to get a few things for the house. Lizzie stayed with me. We'd already colored four pages and completed a puzzle, and now she was on me about fishing again. I told her I would take her fishing in a couple of weeks and that I had a special surprise for her when we did go. I knew she would be so excited to see the freshwater jellyfish Landon had told me about. She was getting inpatient about waiting, though. Patience was not a virtue any members of my family had.

I told Lizzie I was going to give Milah Jo a call and then we would play Candy Land. Lizzie was watching TV when I slipped out the back door to make my call; I didn't want Lizzie to over-hear me talking about Landon. Milah Jo and I were discussing plans for the weekend. We were going camping with some of Landon's friends and we were trying to get our story straight for what we were going to tell Mother.

When I got off the phone with Milah Jo, I went back inside to start a mean game of Candy Land. But Lizzie wasn't watching TV. I figured she was in the bathroom so I sat down on the couch to wait for her. After a few minutes of quiet, I decided to go check on her. Anybody who knows little kids knows that when they're being quiet, they're usually up to no good. Lizzie wasn't in the bathroom, our room, or Mother's room. It didn't take long for me to search our little house. It also didn't take long for me to start freaking out. It wasn't like Lizzie to just take off. She wasn't in the house, so that meant she had to be outside. I yelled for her a few times, but she didn't answer.

I was so upset that I was freezing and shaking and had tremors going completely through my body. I should have been in the house, because then I would have known where Lizzie was. Where could she have gone? I had stepped out the back door for only about ten minutes to talk to Milah Jo on the phone. How freaking selfish I was! I should have just focused on Lizzie and nothing else—not Landon, not Milah Jo, no one.

I'd been so worried Mother wouldn't take good care of Lizzie, and now I'd failed her also. I called Mother, but she didn't answer so I ended up leaving her a hysterical message that Lizzie was missing. I stepped out into the driveway and started frantically calling for Lizzie.

Landon appeared from behind his house.

"Jane, what's wrong? Why are you yelling for Lizzie?"

"Landon, I was only outside for a few minutes and I came back in and she was gone. Where would she go?" I cried.

"Jane, calm down. We'll find her. Where did you see her last?"

"She was in the living room watching TV. I stepped out the back door to call Milah Jo. When I came back in, Lizzie was gone."

Landon pulled me into a hug, saying, "She's got to be around here somewhere. We'll find her, I promise."

I pulled away.

"How can you be so sure?"

He grabbed my hand and assured me, "I just know. Come on, she can't be far. Did she give you any idea of where she would have gone?"

"I don't know. She was mad at me because I wouldn't take her fishing."

Then it hit me.

"Oh, no! Oh, no! Oh, no! Oh my God! You don't think she would go to the pond by herself, do you? Hurry! Maybe she hasn't made it that far yet!" I screamed.

I was so scared. Lizzie had no idea how to swim; neither one of us did. Landon took off in a sprint toward the pond while I struggled to keep up. He was putting those long legs to good use. There was no way I could stay with him, but I saw Lizzie's little blonde head as soon as I got to the top of the hill. Landon was already headed down the hill toward the pond. Lizzie was almost to the pond, and I yelled for her to stop. She turned, saw Landon gaining on her, and took off running. I yelled for her again, but she didn't turn around this time. She just kept running.

"Hurry, Landon, catch up with her!"

He was getting close to Lizzie, but she made it to the dock and kept running.

"No, Lizzie, no!" I screamed.

Her little foot tripped on one of the boards on the dock, and Lizzie hit her head on the railing. She crumpled to the dock before flopping into the water face-first. My mind went into a frenzy. What was I going to do? I couldn't swim. Just as I'd decided I was going in after her anyway, I heard a splash as Landon hit the water. I made it to the dock just as Landon was reaching Lizzie, who was floating face-down in the water.

It was one of the scariest things I'd ever seen in my life. I was sure that image would become permanently ingrained in my mind.

Landon snatched up Lizzie, and she started coughing. He swam her to the edge of the pond, and I reached down and lifted her out of the water. I stepped a couple of feet away from the pond and fell to the ground with her. My legs were jelly. I could barely hold my own weight, so when I added Lizzie's, my legs went out from underneath me.

Lizzie was crying and saying she was sorry, that she just wanted to go jellyfishing. I yelled at her and told her to never do that to me again. Then I held her so tight I didn't think I could ever let go. I was so relieved she was conscious and breathing.

Landon was completely out of breath and had just sat down next to us when I heard the sirens. In the city you heard sirens all the time, but that was the first time I'd ever heard them out in the boonies.

"Those sirens are getting really close. Did you call 911?" Landon asked me.

"No, I didn't," I replied. "But I did leave Mother an awful voicemail that Lizzie was missing. She must be stroking out by now. I bet she called them. We'd better head back to the house before they send out a whole search party."

I started to get up and realized my legs were still partially out of commission and there was no way I was going to be able to carry Lizzie back to the house. Landon saw me about fall back down and took my sister from my arms. The fire truck and ambulance were pulling up by the house when we came over the hill. We approached the EMTs as they were getting out. We explained to them what had happened and they advised that they should have a look at Lizzie.

Lizzie was in the back of the ambulance when Mother pulled in. She came flying out of the car toward us. I pointed over to the ambulance.

"She's fine. They just wanted to take a look at her to make sure. Did you call 911?" I asked.

Mother was furious.

"Yes, I called 911! You scared the hell out of me, Jane! I tried to call you back several times. Why didn't you answer? What the hell happened?"

She didn't even give me time to answer. She made her way to the ambulance to get Lizzie. I didn't care that she was mad at me. I deserved it. I should have been watching Lizzie better. All that mattered now was that Lizzie was okay. Landon stayed right by me, holding my hand. I tried to convince him to go get some dry clothes on, but he wasn't leaving me alone. He knew I was a wreck. He kept hold of me the whole time we were standing there. He didn't care that my mother saw us, and he didn't care that his mother had arrived and had seen us together also. We were getting some strange looks. Now we would have to explain our relationship, as well as what had just happened.

Mother informed me she was going to ride with Lizzie to the hospital to get X-rays done, since Lizzie might have swallowed some of the pond water. It was probably a good idea since she'd hit her head also. Mother wouldn't let me go with them. She let me know that it would be best if I stayed home. She had no right to treat me that badly. I felt horrible about what had happened and knew that I'd screwed up, but how many times had she left me and Lizzie in danger while she was off getting high somewhere? What made her so righteous all of a sudden?

She was right, though: This was my fault.

Mrs. Whitman and Mother talked for a few minutes before Mrs. Whitman came over to Landon and me to find out what happened. Apparently, she was going to get the scoop before she went to the hospital to pick up Mother and Lizzie. Landon explained the story, but his mom didn't appear to be paying much attention to what he was saying. She seemed to be more interested in staring at Landon's and my hands interlocked together. She gave me a sarcastic thrashing for not paying more attention to Lizzie and informed Landon that it would be best if he went into the house now. Landon put his arm around my waist and told her he thought he would keep me company until they got back with Lizzie. She gave us one heck of a dirty look and left.

Landon and I went into Landon's house so he could get some dry clothes. I told him I would wait in the kitchen for him. It didn't take him long to change. I was standing in front of the window looking out when I felt him wrap his arms around me. He spun me around so I was facing him. He saw the tears running down my cheek and wiped them away.

"Jane, why are you crying? Lizzie is going to be fine. This isn't your fault. It could have happened on anybody's watch. Lizzie saw her opportunity and took it. You said yourself she was determined to go jellyfishing. Everything is okay, I promise."

He hugged me. Even after being in that nasty pond, he smelled so good. How could I be thinking what I was thinking? How could I do it? But how could I not? I pulled away.

"Landon, you can't seriously make this Lizzie's fault," I said. "She's four years old. This is my fault. I was too self-involved to pay attention to her. I shouldn't have left her alone for one second. This is getting out of hand. Lizzie has always been my first priority, not myself and certainly not some guy. As much as I love spending time with you, Landon, I cannot do it anymore. I need to focus on Lizzie. I'm all she has. If she can't count on me to protect her, then she can't count on anyone. I can't do this anymore, Landon."

Landon pulled me close to him again.

"Jane, this is not your fault," he said. "What happened today could have happened if you'd gone into the bathroom for a few minutes. Don't start making excuses about why we can't be together again. You are stuck with me, my dear. I love you."

I pulled away from him and walked to the end of the counter. He'd just said he loved me. It had been so long since someone had told me that they loved me. All I wanted to do was tell him I loved him too, but I couldn't. I had to fight this for Lizzie. She needed me more than I needed Landon.

"Don't do this, Landon.," I said, crying. "It's not going to work. You can have any girl you want. You don't love me."

"You're always pulling away from me, Jane," Landon protested. "Sometimes I feel like I'm talking to a wall. I'm screaming at you that I love you and you look the other way. Can you not hear me, or do you just not love me back?"

I looked down at the floor. Landon would not give up, and I knew soon I would no longer be able to stand my ground. I would once again cave. I needed him too much not to.

He cupped my chin into his hands and raised my face to his.

"Hold your damn head up, girl," he said. "That's it! I'm getting tired of this. Come with me."

He grabbed me by the arm, dragged me up the stairs to his room, and faced me in front of the mirror.

"Look at you—you're beautiful. And if this mirror showed you the way I see you, it would shatter. It could not withstand your beauty. I've never wanted someone the way I want you. Not just physically; I want you here with me in my heart and soul. When I'm without you, I feel like I can't breathe. You literally take my breath away. I cannot live without you now. I spend every moment we're not together obsessing over you. From this moment on, you will never be alone. You have to let me love you. Please, I'm begging you. Why can't you realize you should be loved? You deserve it!"

He turned me around and pulled me as close to his body as we could get without melting into each other. He took my face in his hands again.

"Jane, I will not let you go," he said. "You can fight me with all you've got. I will not let you leave."

He kissed me hard. There was so much fire in that kiss I felt as if I were going to burst into flames. I couldn't fight back anymore. I surrendered. I kissed him back. I knew I loved him. I knew there was no turning back. I would just have to deal with whatever came my way. But at that moment in time, I did not care about what tomorrow was going to bring. I just wanted him today. I just wanted this now.

He pulled away from my lips, shocked that I'd kissed him back that way. He looked into my eyes and flashed me a smile of relief.

When I looked at him, I saw my reflection in his eyes and I could see I was smiling too. How long had it been since I'd felt this way? Never. I'd never felt this way about anyone. I had no idea how to be close to someone like this. I'd spent the last four years distancing myself from anyone who tried to get close to me. And there I was, letting this boy get as close as he wanted. What the hell was I thinking? That was just it: I wasn't thinking at all anymore.

We ended up going back to my little house to wait on Mother, Lizzie, and Mrs. Whitman to get home from the hospital. I had called to check on Lizzie, but I just got Mother's voicemail. Landon and I both knew we were going to get the third degree about what had happened with Lizzie and about us dating. Landon assured me that what happened was just an accident and that Mother would probably be calmed down by the time she made it home. We both agreed that his mom would be pitching a fit about us being together, though. I figured she was going to lay into him pretty good. Probably something about how he could do so much better than me. I knew she definitely didn't see me as good enough to date her son. Landon didn't seem to care what she thought, thankfully.

We were hanging out watching TV when Mother got home. Lizzie came running in the door and ran up to Landon.

"Thanks, Wandon, for saving me from the water. It was deep. Mommy said to say thank you."

Landon smiled at her.

"You're welcome, short stuff. I'm glad you're okay."

Lizzie returned the smile. "Yeah, I okay. The doctor taked a picture of my bones."

Mother chimed in and thanked Landon also. Landon kissed me on the cheek and went back to his house. He told me he would catch up with me tomorrow. Mother flashed me strange looks after Landon kissed me and Lizzie let out a big, "Oooohhh, yuck!" I couldn't help but laugh at her. I grabbed ahold of her and held her tight to me. I was so grateful she was okay.

"Jane, I'm sorry I was so upset with you earlier," Mother said. "I was very worried about Lizzie. What happened was an accident and could have happened no matter who was watching her. Let's just hope Children Services doesn't get wind of what happened. That is something they'd want to check out. I would really like to keep them away from us. I'm so tired of them thinking they can run our lives. Everything is as it should be now, and I don't want them screwing with us anymore."

I couldn't do anything but stare at Mother. She had to be freaking kidding me! After all she'd put me and Lizzie through, she had the nerve to worry about *me* doing something to screw it up? She was the one running around with her NA buddies all the time. Who knew what she was out doing with them? She made me so damn mad. Who did she think she was, talking like it's all Children Services's fault that our lives had been so messed up? She was the one who'd screwed up everything. Not them and certainly not me.

Mother did ask about Landon and me. I just told her we were getting to be friends and left it at that. She didn't need to know my business. I gave Lizzie a big hug, told her I was very happy she was okay, and hit the shower so I could go to bed. I didn't want to deal with Mother any more that night.

I didn't sleep very well, though. Every time I closed my eyes, I saw Lizzie underwater, looking up at me for help. That wasn't how it had really happened, but it was definitely how my mind was deciding to process it. I couldn't handle it. I ended up reading most of the night. I think it was around 4 a.m. when I realized I couldn't hold my eyes open anymore. I crawled in bed with Lizzie and cradled her in my arms until morning, when she woke up and told me to get off her. At least I managed to get a little sleep when I had her safe in my arms.

Lessons

I woke up hoping the day would be uneventful. I definitely didn't want any more accidents or surprises any time soon. I'd managed to keep it secret that it was my sixteenth birthday—secret from everyone except Mother, of course. I didn't want anyone to make a big deal out of it. I wasn't used to a big fuss and I didn't want one now. Lizzie knew, though. She wished me a happy birthday first thing in the morning. That meant Mother must have told her. I'd really been hoping she would just forget about it.

Lizzie and I went into the kitchen to get some breakfast, and there was a gift box on the counter with a card that read "Jane." I sighed and opened the card. It was a really sappy card signed by Mother and Lizzie. In the bottom corner Mother had written, "You will never know how much I really do love you. You are so special to me." Lizzie was jumping up and down wanting me to open the gift box. I did and was shocked to see it was a cell phone. I couldn't help but be excited. I'd wanted a phone for a long time but just figured it would never happen.

When I turned it on, I saw I already had two text messages. The first one was from Mother and read, "Jane, send Lizzie over at noon and go to the garage. She can spend the day helping me and you can enjoy your day. Happy Birthday, Baby. Love, Mom." Why in the world would she want me to go to the garage? It might have been my sixteenth birthday, but I knew she didn't have the money to buy me a car. She needed to get herself a better one first.

Lizzie and I ate our breakfast and went to get dressed. I was almost done getting us ready when I remembered there was a second text on the phone. I grabbed it to see what else Mother had to say. The text wasn't from her, though; it was from Landon. Mother must have given him my number that morning. His text said, "Hey, City Girl! Make sure you grab ur suit and towel. We be hittin the beach 2day."

What the heck was he thinking? I couldn't swim. He knew that, and why in the world would I want to go anywhere near water after what had happened just a few days ago? I shrugged my shoulders and opened my drawer to get my suit. Lizzie giggled when I pulled a brand-new swimsuit out of the drawer. I have to say I was relieved, because the only suit I had was a dingey old thing that had those little lint balls all over the butt. The suit Mother had gotten me was really cool. It was a black bikini with a white skull and crossbones on one side of the front. I loved it.

I wasn't sure how Mother had known Landon would be taking me swimming when she hadn't even known about me and Landon until the other day. Or, maybe she *had* already known about us and I'd just thought we were keeping it a secret.

I walked Lizzie over to the Whitmans' house and then headed to the garage. Landon was waiting for me inside. He looked so hot standing there next to his car with his ripped-up jeans, white T-shirt, and a bandanna wrap on his head. I don't know what it is about that bad-boy look, but it worked for him. It was freaking hot. He was getting really good at making me swoon.

He smiled at me.

"It's about time, City Girl. You're late."

I couldn't help but smile back at him.

"You've got to give a girl a break," I said. "These plans were sprung on me at the last minute. I thought I got ready pretty fast considering you're taking me swimming so soon after my little sister about drowned on my watch. What are you thinking?"

He grabbed my hand and pulled me close to him.

"I'm not being insensitive. I think you need to learn how to swim, girl," he said. "I figured you would feel better about having Lizzie around water if you knew how. We don't have to go if you don't want to. I understand."

I was a little shocked. I hadn't thought about it like that, but he was right. I did need to learn to swim. Had I known how to swim, I wouldn't have felt so helpless the other day. It wasn't that I was scared of the water or didn't want to learn. I just really had never had the opportunity to go swimming. Most foster homes never had pools, nor would the foster parents take us on family outings.

I folded my arms across my chest.

"Just what makes you think you're qualified to teach someone how to swim, anyway?"

Landon laughed at me.

"Always the skeptic, aren't you, Jane? Well, for your information, I spent last summer as a lifeguard. I think I can handle it."

Of course he could. What *couldn't* he do? We loaded up the car and set out to the beach. We were almost to the end of the driveway when I realized I had no idea where the beach was around there. Did he mean the Beach Waterpark or some makeshift beach at a lake somewhere?

I turned toward him and asked, "Landon, where is it exactly that we're going swimming?"

"There's a pretty good beach about an hour from here," he said. "I know it's a little bit of a drive, but it's a big beach that's shallow a good ways out. It would be a good place to learn to swim. The only downfall is that it's always crowded on hot days."

I scrunched my nose.

"I'm not real sure I'm up for an audience to watch me make a fool of myself. Is there anywhere else we could go?"

I felt like I was being a pain in the butt, but I really wanted to go somewhere more private.

Landon gave me that award-winning smile of his.

"Why are you always so worried about the people around you all the time?" he asked. "Jane, you're a wonderful person and you shouldn't be so concerned with what people think of you. What do any of their opinions matter anyway?

"There's a place over by Seaman. We call it the swirl hole. It's a deep part of Brush Creek. We could go there, but it's pretty deep. You'd have to either sink or swim," he said, chuckling.

I frowned.

"A creek? Aren't there snakes and fish and stuff in those?"

Landon laughed out loud.

"Yes, but all those are in that beach we were going to go to also."

I scratched my head.

"Oh, that's so gross! I don't know if I like the idea of swimming with creepy crawlers. I guess I don't have a choice about that, though. Don't you know anybody with a pool?"

Landon looked like he was starting to get frustrated with me.

"I could probably find one, but you would have an audience," he said. "You can't have it both ways. You're going to have to choose between the audience or the snakes and fish."

I frowned again.

"That's not much of a choice. I guess it's the snakes and the fish. At least they can't laugh at me."

Landon turned left out of the driveway and headed toward Seaman. The swirl hole wasn't too far away; we were there in about fifteen minutes. Landon had failed to tell me we would have to walk a mile through a field of weeds to get to the water. I was so worried about those tick bug things getting on me and sucking my blood. That's just disgusting. I'd seen one on a dog one time and it was huge. Landon just laughed at me and said he would be sure to check me over really good.

The day turned out to be wonderful despite all the creepy crawlers in the weeds and in the water. Being that close to Landon the whole time we were in the water seemed to help me take my mind off the other stuff. I did actually learn to be comfortable in the water. I could tread water and go under. Landon was a wonderful teacher. He showed off a few times by swinging off this old rope that was hanging from a tree on the other side of the creek. I could never do that, no matter how well I learned to swim. I couldn't imagine how deep he went under after he fell from that rope.

My favorite part of the day was when we were resting on the blanket Landon had brought. We lay back on it, held onto each other, and talked the whole time. Well, maybe not the whole time. There might have been some kissing involved. Landon was a great kisser. Not that I had much to compare it to. I hadn't kissed any other guys, unless you counted Bo Robbins in first grade. Landon's lips were always so warm and his arms were always wrapped around me. I loved it when he cradled my face with his hands or when he slid his hands down my neck and back. It gave me chills just to think about it.

Little green monsters

The rest of the week went pretty quickly. I was excited and completely freaked out about going camping that coming weekend. There was this huge Battle of the Bands thing going on a couple towns over in Manchester. It was down by the Ohio River. Maybe I would feel more comfortable there since I was used to being around the river in Cincinnati. Landon assured me we would have a good time. Part of me wished Milah Jo was going, especially since she was lying to Mother about me staying the weekend with her. I didn't want her to feel like I was using her. I would never do that to her. Milah Jo had proved to be a great friend, and of course she was more than happy to go along with it. She loved the idea of me and Landon together.

Mother dropped me off at Milah Jo's on Saturday morning. I'd been a little worried that she would want to talk to Milah Jo's mom, but she was in a hurry to get her errands done so she just dropped me off. I dropped my bag by the bushes after Mother pulled away. Milah Jo's grandparents thought I was visiting for just a few hours. It would have looked bad if I'd come in carrying a bag and then left with Landon later. Landon was picking me up at two, so I would have a few hours with Milah Jo. We spent most of the morning in her room talking about the upcoming night. She kept questioning me about my virginity and if I was going to do anything with Landon. I confessed that I was a virgin and that I'd fallen in love with Landon, but I would not make any of the mistakes Mother had. I told Milah Jo that I was not ready for sex and had no intentions of letting things get that far. Milah Jo being Milah Jo, she just kept telling me I really couldn't say that until I was in the heat of the moment. She was convinced that since I'd never been in that position before, I couldn't possibly say I would say no. All morning, everything I heard was, "Girl, you're crazy about that boy and I honestly don't think you could refuse him anything now. I know I couldn't." Then she would just giggle.

It was no secret between me and Milah Jo that she thought Landon was *hot*! But she'd developed a new crush on Jackson Jenkins right before school had let out for the summer. She'd been doing everything she could to get his attention and was mad that it was summer and she couldn't see him anymore. She was pretty happy, though, when Landon told her he had known Jackson since kindergarten and that he would see what he could do about setting up a date. I hoped Landon could work his magic, because Milah Jo was already over the moon about the idea of it.

I started getting really nervous as two o'clock approached. What if Landon *did* expect me to have sex with him that night? I was so worried that he would dump me if I didn't put out. How could I be so excited and scared about the same thing? My feelings always seemed to be so complex. Nothing ever seemed to be black or white. It was always grey.

Landon was right on time. I snuck my bag into his car, and he leaned over to kiss me as soon as I got in. He smiled that amazing smile and asked me if I was ready to have some fun. I assured him I was, but I wasn't too sure I was very convincing. I stared out the car window for most of the ride. After about twenty minutes, he asked me if something was wrong.

I turned toward him and frowned, saying, "I just can't seem to hide my feelings from you."

He laughed.

"Jane, you can't hide your feelings from me. Your face and body language always show what you're feeling. You may think you hide your feelings from everybody, but you don't. Not to mention you haven't said two words the whole drive. Now, tell me what you're so worried about."

Ugh! How did that boy know me so well? I had known him for only a few months and he already had me figured out. So, after a couple minutes of trying to decide what to do, I just spilled it. I figured that would work better, because if he got mad, then he could just go ahead and take me home right then. Before I knew it, I'd blurted it out: "Landon, I cannot have sex with you tonight, so I hope that's not what you have planned."

Landon frowned at me.

"Really, Jane, is that what's bothering you? Do you think that's why I invited you camping?" he asked. "I do believe we've spent other nights together without having sex. Why would you think that now? I'm hurt, Jane. I love and respect you so much. I would never ask you to do anything you're not ready for. Hell, you just turned sixteen this week. I wouldn't expect you to be ready for that yet. I'm not like that, Jane. Holding you in my arms all night is all I want. You mean more to me than just sex."

I felt relief and guilt wash over me at the same time. I was relieved he wasn't expecting more from me than I was ready to give, but I felt guilty I'd assumed that was what he had wanted. I think he was upset with me.

Maybe someday I would feel secure enough in our relationship to realize Landon really did love and respect me. I sighed.

"I'm sorry, Landon," I said. "I was just so worried that you would expect more tonight since we've gotten so close lately. I didn't mean to upset you."

Landon reached over and grabbed my hand.

"I'm not upset with you," he assured me. "I understand where you're coming from. Someday you'll realize I love you for you and not for what I can get from you. Now, are you ready to have some fun tonight? You should relax. I know you'll enjoy these bands. They're totally your kind of music."

He was completely right. The bands were awesome. I finally got to see that local band, Rootbound, that everybody talked about. They were great. I couldn't believe how fantastic they were. Landon bought me one of their T-shirts from the merch tent. I didn't like him buying me things, but I really did want that shirt. Landon stayed right by my side almost all night. I think he might have wandered off once to talk to a few older-looking guys. He was so attentive. I'd never had anybody pay that much attention to me in my whole life.

The only downside to the night was that there were a few girls from school who decided to blurt out "Freak!" whenever they walked by me. I tried not to let them get to me anymore. They could say what they wanted. I wasn't going to let them ruin my night. Landon, on the other hand, decided to let them have it. I had never seen that side of him. I hated that he was drawing more attention to me, but at the same time it felt really good to hear someone take up for me like that.

Thank goodness we'd gotten there early in the day. Landon had gone ahead and put the tent up. He'd found a great spot that was a little farther from everyone else. He'd raised his eyebrows up and down and smiled real big at me when we were putting the tent up. "Privacy," he'd said.

I gave him an eyebrow up and a not-so-nice smile. He just laughed at me and said, "For when you have to tinkle. Get your mind out of the gutter, City Girl."

We both burst out laughing. Landon was always so fun and easygoing, but that night he was even more enjoyable than usual. It was like he was just cutting loose. I had the best time with him.

I awoke the next morning listening to the birds singing and felt happier than I could have ever imagined. Spending the entire night with Landon's arms around me had been pure bliss. I'd slept better that night than I had in years. I'd been sure Landon was going to be upset with me for not having sex with him, but he wasn't. He was completely understanding about it. He said we would know when the time was right for those kinds of things to take place. Instead, we had kissed and held each other half the night and then fallen asleep in each other's arms. It didn't matter that we were sleeping on the ground in a cold, damp tent. I'd been perfectly comfortable the entire night, but now I had to pee, or "tinkle," as Landon had put it. I hated to climb out of his arms, but nature was calling.

When I slipped out of the blanket, I realized it was pretty chilly for a July morning. I looked around and saw Landon's jacket in the corner of the tent. I grabbed it and put it on. It was a little oversized for me, but it would work. I unzipped the tent and stepped out of it. I looked around to see where would be a good place to go. We had put our tent a good distance from everyone else's tents, so I was sure nobody would see me. I saw two bushy-looking plants over to the left of the tent about twenty feet away, so I stuck my hands in my pockets and started walking.

As I was walking, I felt something in Landon's jacket pocket and pulled it out to see what it was. It was a small green pill with an "80" on one side and "OC" on the other side. I instantly knew what I had in my hand. All the reading and research I had done on the subject told me exactly what it was. It was an 80mg OxyContin.

My knees buckled, and I fell to the ground. This couldn't be. There had to be some kind of mistake. This couldn't be Landon's jacket. But I knew it was his jacket. Maybe someone else had worn it at the bonfire. There was no way this pill could be his.

My mind was reeling with ideas about how drugs could have gotten into Landon's jacket and reasons why Landon would have pills. This didn't make sense. I knew the symptoms of drug use, and Landon didn't show any of them. Maybe someone had offered it to him last night and he'd taken it so he wouldn't seem rude. That had to be it. I headed straight back to the tent to ask him about it.

When I unzipped the front of the tent and stepped in, Landon was lying flat on his back with his hands behind his head. His beautiful smile lit up the whole tent, and that smile was for me. Wow—there was no way he had anything to do with the OC I found in his jacket. He was just too perfect. Maybe I shouldn't even bring it up. I didn't want him to think I was accusing him of anything. The last thing I wanted was for that stupid pill to come between us. I had fallen completely in love with Landon Whitman, and I didn't want him to think I didn't trust him. I shouldn't be suspicious of him.

He was lying there with a puzzled look on his face. I was worried he knew what I'd found in his jacket pocket. I looked down and asked, "What's wrong?"

He answered, "How could anything be wrong after I spent the entire night with you in my arms? I'm amazed that you're even more beautiful in the morning after an entire night in this musty old tent."

"Are you kidding me?" I responded. "I was perfectly comfy last night. I slept better last night than I had in a long time. I could have slept on sharp rocks and felt like I was in heaven as long as I was in your arms."

He laughed. He had such a wonderful laugh.

"You give me too much credit," Landon said. "I don't think I could make sharp rocks comfy."

I smiled. I decided I would keep what I'd found to myself. I wouldn't even mention it. I took his jacket off and put it back in the corner where I'd found it. I crawled into the blanket and wedged myself back into Landon's arms. He hugged me tightly to his body and I felt a twinge go through my entire being. I felt it in my body and my soul. When he touched me, it felt like magic. Every doubt I'd had was gone. The thought that that pill was his had been wiped away.

"So, Mr. Whitman, what's the plan for today?"

His left eyebrow went down and he made a strange face as he replied, "Mr. Whitman is my father. You really shouldn't call me that; it sounds kind of weird."

We ended up spending that entire day together and just about every other day that followed for the rest of the summer. I could feel myself becoming happier and happier with each passing day. I was starting to forget what life had been like before I'd met Landon. I'd totally let him in. My walls were completely down. I was absolutely sure Landon was the love of my life, the soulmate I'd been waiting for without realizing I'd been waiting for him. It was so scary to think about not having him in my life. Mother had better not ruin this for me. Leaving then would have devastated me for sure.

The truth hurts

Milah Jo got her permit in August and was very nervous about taking her driver's test when she was finished with driver's education. She was so nervous, she'd taken up smoking. I hadn't even messed with getting my permit since I knew we didn't have the money for driver's ed. Landon always took me wherever I needed to go anyway, so it wasn't really a priority. For Milah Jo, a driver's license meant freedom, and she couldn't wait for that. She was still trying to figure out what she was going to be driving to find that freedom, though.

School started right back up where it had left off—with me being the freak. I'd hoped that since I wasn't the new kid anymore, maybe I'd be treated like a normal person. That didn't happen. I was pretty sure Emily was ticked that Landon and I were still together and she was going to make sure everybody knew just how infuriated she was. She and Mrs. Whitman had both expressed their disapproval of mine and Landon's relationship. I believed that when it came right down to it, neither one of them could handle the thought of Landon dating someone who'd come from nothing. I wasn't good enough for him. Sometimes I wondered if they were right.

Mother hadn't said a whole lot about me dating Landon. I could tell she was worried it would affect her job, though. I'd told her not to worry, that I wouldn't do anything to screw up her masquerade of a cute little perfect home. She might have had everybody else fooled, but I knew she was a pretender. She would screw up sooner or later, and then Lizzie and I would be the ones to pay the price.

School had been getting worse than usual. Landon had been slacking in his school work, and I didn't know what he was thinking. This was his senior year and he was blowing it. He just didn't seem interested in doing anything for school. It was strange, because Landon had been a really good student. Emily wouldn't let up. She'd started ragging on me with full force at the beginning of the year and was still going strong. One day, Milah Jo had come charging down the hall where my locker was located with that "I'm going to take somebody out" look all over her face again. She approached me completely out of breath.

"Milah Jo, you really need to quit smoking, then maybe the short distance down the hall wouldn't leave you so breathless," I told her.

She gave me an angry look and hissed, "That Emily Whitman is at it again. She's got a whole crowd together by the gym telling them all kinds of stuff about you. She told them you got kicked out of your old school because you'd slept with so many guys. I'm sure she made it up, but those stupid people are eating it up like she's preaching to a congregation. She's gotta be stopped."

I just shrugged it off.

"Milah Jo, I can't do anything about what Emily says about me. Besides, if everybody is stupid enough to believe what she has to say, then that's their problem. Not mine and not yours. You need to calm down or you're going to end up getting yourself into trouble."

Milah Jo threw her hands on her hips.

"Jane, you really need to stop letting people treat you so ugly!" She stomped off. She was definitely upset with me.

When we sat down at lunch that day, Landon never even mentioned the rumors Emily had been spreading. I knew he had to have heard what was being said. I didn't know if he was afraid of upsetting me or if he didn't say anything because he'd been so distracted lately. I really couldn't figure out what was up with him, but I was going to make sure to ask him.

I was starting to get worried. I could have sworn he'd lost a few pounds in the last few weeks. He'd said he had a stomach bug and hadn't had much of an appetite lately. Last weekend, when we'd gone to the movies, we'd stopped at the pines afterward. We were just talking, and the next thing I knew he was asleep while I was talking to him. I could have sworn he'd nodded off during the movie also. He just said he was really tired from working on Kyle's dad's farm.

I never got to ask Landon what was up with him. He seemed to be getting pretty good at avoiding me after school. He was always working with Kyle, which made no sense because the boy sure didn't have a need for money. He already had some kind of trust fund or something. Things were just getting more and more outlandish as the days went by.

• • • • •

I should have seen it coming. I guess love really does make you blind. How I'd just let all the signs slip right past me was beyond me. So, I just lay there in my bed in the fetal position. I felt like I couldn't move. I felt numb except for the constant shaking that would not go away. What was I supposed to do now? I didn't want to deal with this. I didn't understand how it had been going on all this time and I hadn't even seen it. Sure, I'd seen some of the signs, but I just couldn't believe he would ever do something like that. Not my Landon. I ignored the signs because I didn't want to make accusations against someone I loved so much. *Not my Landon.* He loved me too much. At least, he said he loved me. How could he love me and do what he'd been doing?

I could feel that he was standing in the doorway of my bedroom. He must have come in the back door after Mother and Lizzie had left. I knew he was there. I could feel his presence. I could always feel his presence. After our conversation that morning, I really didn't understand why he would even want to be there. He point blank had told me he didn't want to quit. Evidently he didn't love me enough to quit. That was the story of my life: The people I loved all loved drugs more than they loved me. He didn't want to quit, he didn't want to lose me, and he wanted me to accept it. He wanted me to be okay with it. He said he didn't do it that much and that he could keep it under control.

I'd been in multiple foster homes because someone couldn't keep it under control. No one can keep it under control. It's an ugly monster that feeds off innocent lives. It sucks them in, takes them under, and then destroys them and the people who love them.

"Jane, please talk to me," Landon said. "You need to listen to me. It's no big deal really. I only do it every now and then. I've done it the whole time you've known me. It doesn't change anything. It's not like I'm blowing a huge hole in my nose. I don't understand why you're so upset. It's just a few pills. I don't do heroin. I'm not shooting anything, and I never would. I hate needles."

I did not turn around; I just lay there. I didn't want to hear anymore. But deep down, I knew I didn't want him to leave either. I needed him. He was one of the biggest reasons I smiled since I'd moved here. He was the reason I didn't complain about living in the middle of nowhere anymore. He was the reason I got up for school ready to go. He was the reason I felt alive and not like that zombie that was walking around going through the motions of life before I'd come here.

I heard him coming closer. He sat down at the end of my bed. He knew Mother and Lizzie wouldn't be back for a few hours. They'd gone to the park about an hour ago and they usually stayed for a while. He must not have been planning to leave any time soon.

My shaking was slowing down, but the numbness was still there. Why did my limbs feel so heavy? I should have known this had been too good to be true. Something this good couldn't last. Why had I even thought it would? This was me, after all—nothing in my life was ever permanent. Everything was always temporary and damaged. This relationship was not any different. But damn, couldn't he have cheated on me? I probably could have handled that better than this. This went straight to my heart. This was the one thing in my life that seemed to constantly mess it up. It would have made sense if I'd been the one doing it, but I wasn't. I'd never touched that stuff, yet it always seemed to creep into my life and wreak havoc.

I lay there replaying the events of the morning in my head. I'd gotten ready for school early, and I knew no one but Landon was home at his house. Emily was skipping school once again to go shopping at the outlet mall an hour away. So, I snuck into the house. I went in through the back door and quietly went up the stairs to Landon's room. I wanted to surprise him and wake him up. He was always telling me to be more spontaneous and live on the edge a little. I thought sneaking into Mrs. Whitman's house and into Landon's bedroom constituted living on the edge, considering Mrs. Whitman hated me. I was so excited. We would have a good hour before we'd have to leave for school. I was ready to show Landon how spontaneous I could be.

I opened the door to his bedroom to find he wasn't in his bed. I looked around the room and headed for his bathroom door. At first, I thought I'd better not rush in. He could have been going to the restroom, and that would have been totally embarrassing. So I waited, and waited, and waited. After about ten minutes, I started to get worried so I knocked on the door. There was no answer, so I decided to open the bathroom door and suffer the consequences.

When I first opened the door, I was terrified. There was Landon sitting on the toilet all slumped over, drool hanging from his mouth. He was completely out of it. I shook him to try to wake him up, but I couldn't. I shook him again. Nothing. I knelt down and lifted his face even with mine. When I looked at him, I knew what was wrong. There was this gunky white stuff coming out of his nose. I shoved his face out of my hands and scooted back against the wall. I must have shoved him with a little more force than I'd intended, because he fell over and hit his head on the sink. That woke him up. He raised his head and looked around the room in a daze. By this time, I'd slid down the wall and was on the floor beside the tub.

He looked at me and asked groggily, "Jane, wh--, what are you doing here?"

"Trying to surprise you!" I snapped.

"Why are you in my bathroom?" he sputtered.

"You were nodded out in here. This is where I found you," I answered.

"I must have fallen asleep. I was so tired from working with Kyle yesterday."

"Don't even try to tell me you were so tired that you fell asleep on the toilet," I growled. "Do you think I'm that stupid? I see it. The evidence is right there on your face. Why don't you take a look into that mirror and see the leftovers coming out of your nose? Careful now, you might be able to save that and snort it later. It looks pretty potent."

Landon stood up slowly and leaned over the sink to look in the mirror. He grabbed a tissue and wiped his nose. He just stood there looking in the mirror. I didn't move. We stayed like that for about fifteen minutes. The whole time, I was running through everything I'd seen over the past six months: the pill in his jacket pocket, the falling asleep in the middle of our conversations, and the weight he'd lost. I knew. I *so* knew. I'd stayed in denial. I hadn't wanted to even consider the thought that Landon was using drugs. I'd just kept telling myself that I was paranoid to love someone and that I was just seeing the signs of use because I was looking so hard for them in my mother. Now, the proof was right in front of my face and I couldn't deny it anymore.

Landon finally spoke.

"Yeah, Kyle gave me something last night to keep me going so I could study for my chemistry test," he said. "It must have been stronger than I thought to knock me out. Sorry, I didn't mean for you to see me like that."

"Why would you do something like that? Don't you know how dangerous that is?" I asked, seething. "Since when do you worry about studying for a test? You haven't been interested in your schoolwork at all this year, and doing that stuff sure didn't keep you going. It knocked your ass out. I was scared to death. I thought something was seriously wrong with you, Landon."

"It was only a Percocet," he responded. "It wasn't anything major. I take them sometimes. Why are you so pissed?"

I was furious. He takes them sometimes? It isn't anything major? Only a Percocet? How could he be so casual about it, acting as if it were something I should have already known? But I guess I *had* already known, hadn't I? I just sat there glaring at his reflection in the mirror. He had to see the disgust in my face.

Landon turned around and bent down to where I was sitting.

"Why are you looking at me like that? You look like you're getting ready to go bipolar, Jane. Don't tell me you didn't know."

"I didn't know, Landon," I protested. "We've never once talked about drugs. There were times I thought you might be on something, but I thought I was just being paranoid. I couldn't bring myself to believe you would be involved in anything like that."

"Jane, it's no big deal. I don't do it every day. Come on, don't be so judgmental. Let's get ready for school. We're going to be late."

I stood up.

"I'm not riding to school with you," I said. "You shouldn't even be driving. I refuse to ride with anyone who's as doped up as you are. I'll take the bus."

I stomped out of the bathroom and into his room. He caught up with me by the door and grabbed my arm. I turned and looked him directly in the eye.

"Don't touch me. Don't ever touch me again," I warned.

"What? Why are you being like this?" Landon asked. "You act like I've done something to harm you. This isn't about you, Jane. This is my business, and I don't understand why you're being such a bitch about it."

I pulled away from him and he let go of my arm.

"Why don't you ask my mother and her dope dealer the reason I'm such a bitch about it, Landon?"

I stormed out of his room and flew down the steps. I was amazed I could even make it out of the house. I felt like I was in shock. I'm sure that's what being in shock has to feel like. I took off running down the lane toward the bus stop. I didn't stop until I'd made it to the end of the lane. I felt like I couldn't breathe. I don't know if it was from the running, from the shock of seeing Landon like that, or from the fact that he called me a bitch. Of course, with my luck, the bus came early, so I was completely winded when I had to get on it. I climbed onto the bus and took my old seat next to the red-headed boy. He gave me a horrified look.

"Are you okay?" he asked.

"I'm fine," I answered.

"All righty then," he responded sarcastically.

I was so upset and the stupid smell on the bus was irritating me. I looked over at the red-headed boy and asked, "What is that stinking smell anyway?"

He looked at me and replied, "The bus driver has a pig farm and the bus sits in the middle of the pig farm all day."

I could feel everyone staring at me. It was just like the first time I'd ridden this bus. But this time, I really didn't care as much that they were staring. All I could think about was Landon and the way he'd looked when I found him. It was a flashback to when I'd found Mother after she'd overdosed. It was the feeling of being so scared, you think your heart is going to jump right out of your chest, that weak feeling in your knees like you're going to fall to the ground, and that sick feeling in the pit of your stomach that makes you think you're going to vomit all over everything.

The rest of the day was a fog. I walked around in a daze. I'd left my backpack at Landon's house, so I didn't even have half of my books. But it wouldn't have mattered. I couldn't concentrate. Landon found me at lunch and tried to talk to me, but I got up and just walked away. Milah Jo looked at me so weirdly. She'd been asking me all day what was wrong, but I wasn't coming out with any information. I didn't want to talk about it. I think she might have been getting aggravated with me. I just wanted to get through the day so I could go home, go to bed, shut my eyes, and forget any of this bullshit had happened.

It was such a relief to hear the last bell of the day. Then I could go home and not have to look at another living soul. I needed to be left alone in my own torment and solitude. Mother and Lizzie had plans to go to the park, so I figured they would head out not long after I got home. Landon was waiting for me right by the side entrance of the school. He tried to persuade me to ride home with him. I refused. I wouldn't stop walking, so he got right in front of me.

"Move, Landon. I'm going to miss my bus," I demanded.

"Jane, please just ride home with me," he begged. "We didn't get to finish talking this morning and I can see you're still upset."

I stopped.

"Landon, I don't want to go with you and I sure don't want to talk to you. Besides, why would you want a bipolar bitch in your car anyway?"

He tried to put his arms around me. I flinched and backed away from him.

"I told you not to ever touch me again, you arrogant ass."

He came toward me. I took off walking not realizing I was headed toward the parking lot instead of where the buses were. Landon caught up with me quickly and stepped in front of me again.

"I'm so sorry, Jane," he said. "I shouldn't have said those things. You really caught me off guard. I just couldn't understand why you were making a huge deal out of this. I was upset that you were so angry with me."

"You don't understand why I would be so angry with you?" I asked. "Do you not know what you're doing to yourself? You could have overdosed and died for all I knew. To see you like that was one of the most terrifying moments of my life. There were two other terrifying moments in my life, Landon. Do you want to know what they were? You were with me for one of them, when Lizzie fell in the pond. You have no idea what the other was. I never told you, because I didn't want you to judge me for something that was not my fault. I truly believed that if you knew, you wouldn't want me. My mother overdosed on heroin when Lizzie was four months old. Mother almost died. She survived, but a part of me died that day. The hopeful part of me died. Until I met you, I had no dreams of having a happy and hope-filled life."

"Jane, I didn't know about your mom," Landon said. "I'm so sorry you had to go through that. But that's not going to happen to me. I only take a pill here and there. I don't shoot anything. I would never let it go that far. Please ride home with me. We really need to talk."

"I'm not going with you," I argued. "Move and let me through or I'm going to miss my bus."

"Well, if you miss your bus, then you'll need a ride home, won't you? So, I'm not moving," he added.

"I said move!" I yelled.

The people walking by us were starting to stare, but Landon didn't budge. I thought, *Okay, does he really want to do this here and now? That's fine.* So I asked the question I knew I had to ask:

"Answer me one question, Landon. You're going to have to choose between me and the drugs, because I cannot live in that world again. Are you going to quit?"

I really didn't want to know the answer to that. How rejected I would feel if he were to choose the drugs over me!

"No, no, no, I don't do ultimatums, Jane," he answered. "I don't have to choose. This is who I am. This is who you fell in love with. I don't want to stop. I'm young; this is what teenagers do. It's not like it's affecting my life. I work and I go to school. I'm not your mom, Jane. You need to accept me the way I am. I'm sure one day I'll stop, but not right now. This is when I'm supposed to party. Why are you being such a prude?"

Well, there it was: the answer I didn't want. I could feel my eyes filling with water. The anger had finally turned to hurt. I couldn't hold the tears back. They were coming full force now. I couldn't accept it. I knew better. How could I be with him knowing he was ruining any chance of a future we would have? I finally looked him in the eye.

"Landon, I'm walking away now. DO NOT FOLLOW ME. Let me go."

I went out around him and headed for the buses. I looked up to see my bus pulling away. Great! Now what was I going to do? I just kept walking out toward the soccer field. I felt like my feet were going to fall out from under me. I had to sit down. I found a tree by the concession stand and sat down with my head between my knees and bawled. I cried until I didn't think I had any liquid left in my body. I finally realized Mother would be wondering where I was. Not that I normally cared so much if she was worried; I just wanted to make sure she and Lizzie would still go to the park. I wanted my time alone. So I took out my phone and called Mother. I told her I'd gone back to get something out of my locker, I'd missed my bus, and I would find a ride home.

Now, I had to find that ride home. I decided to start walking and thumb it. I'd barely made it past the parking lot when a car pulled up next to me. It was Kyle, Landon's friend. He rolled down the window and asked me if I needed a ride home. I knew Landon had gotten him to hang out at the school and wait to see if I needed a ride. I really didn't want to take it, especially knowing he was the one who had given Landon the pills. But I really wanted to get home. I just wanted to be alone. Ten minutes in Kyle's car and I would get that, so I took his offer. I walked around to get in the passenger side and saw there was a girl in the passenger seat. I hadn't noticed her before. She didn't look familiar. I didn't think she went to our school, because I'd never seen her before. She had short, edgy brown hair and a few visible tattoos. She definitely didn't go to our school. I doubted she went to any school. Even though she was sitting, I could tell she was tall. She was all legs and you could really see them with the Daisy Duke shorts she was wearing. She was really thin and was wearing a tight tank top that showed off her huge boobs. She looked like someone you wouldn't want your boyfriend around, that's for sure. She opened the door and pulled up her seat so I could get in the back. I was buckling my seat belt when Kyle introduced us.

"Jane, this is Ivy, Ivy Lang. She's a friend of mine. Ivy, this is Jane, Landon's girlfriend."

"Oh, really, this is Landon's girlfriend," Ivy sneered. "Landon talks about you all the time. I was wondering when I'd get to meet you. Well, hello then."

"Yeah, hello," I sneered back.

Landon talked about me all the time? Nice. That meant my boyfriend *did* hang around her.

Kyle revved up the engine of his car and took off flying. Great. I might make it home. It was a pretty silent ride. I thought about giving Kyle a good piece of my mind, but I knew it wasn't Kyle's fault. Landon was going to do what he wanted, whether Kyle gave it to him or not. That knowledge didn't make me any less pissed at Kyle, though. I must have made him and Ivy uncomfortable because they barely said two words to each other. It was a very awkward ride.

I was so glad to get out of that car and into my house. I put on my best fake smile for Lizzie as she met me at the door. She wasn't greeting me, though. She was headed for the car and ready to get to the park.

"Geez, Jane. Don't you know I'm going to the park? Get out of my way, woman!" Lizzie said.

"Whoa! Sorry, woman!" I replied.

I smiled at her for real. Only Lizzie could yank a smile out of me now. I headed toward my bed as Mother and Lizzie pulled out of the driveway.

I made it to my bed and shut my eyes, but sleeping just wouldn't happen. My mind was erratic with emotions. I had no idea what I was going to do. I didn't want to lose Landon, but I didn't want to live with the dope either. Been there, done that. It wasn't fun. Besides, I'd been nothing but cold to Mother the last six months because I'd been waiting for her to go back to that stuff. Yet the whole time Landon had been the one doing it, and as mad as I was at him, I didn't feel the hate for him that I did for Mother. How was that possible? How could I explain that? How could you hate one person so much because of her drug use yet love another in spite of his? I knew I still loved Landon. Nothing could ever stop that. Not even dope. But I knew loving him was not enough.

• • • • •

Landon must have gotten tired of sitting in the silence because he finally got up and walked out after about an hour. As soon as I heard the back door slam, the tears came on in full force again. I cried myself into a depressed slumber.

Shut down

The next few weeks were a complete daze. I'd shut down and wasn't talking to anyone, not Landon, not Milah Jo, and not even Lizzie. I couldn't bring myself to deal with anyone. I had to get it together. I didn't want to hurt anyone, especially Lizzie. I just couldn't bring myself to fake it for them. It seemed like it took all the energy I had to get out of bed and shower, let alone talk to people.

Mother had been hounding me for a week to find out what was wrong with me. She said I wasn't being my usual sarcastic self. She seemed genuinely worried about me. Deep down, I was starting to feel a little bad for treating her the way I had. Evidently my judgment had been seriously flawed. I'd been cruel to her all this time because I was scared to death she was going to let me down, and the one person I'd put all my faith into ended up destroying me. I promised myself from that moment on I would ease up on Mother. I wasn't going to let her in completely, but I wouldn't make her miserable anymore either. That would be good for all of us, especially Lizzie. I just had to get it together first.

I also decided it was time to open up to Milah Jo. She'd been a really good friend to me and I'd shunned her for the past two weeks. I called her to see if she would pick me up for school. She'd gotten her license the previous week, and I hadn't even congratulated her. She happily agreed to pick me up. She was really excited to show me the car her grandparents had bought her for passing her driver's test. It was a 1976 Volkswagen Beetle. It was multicolored and horrible-looking, but Milah Jo absolutely loved it. I didn't blame her. It had to be nice for her to have something of her very own.

She didn't question me at all on the ride to school. That was very strange for Milah Jo. She did tell me she was very worried about me and that she hoped I would trust her enough to talk to her. I couldn't stand it anymore. I spilled the whole story to her.

Milah Jo gave me that "I'm so sorry" smile and said, "Hon, I would have never dreamed that Landon was doing anything like that. That stupid-ass idiot! What in the world is wrong with that boy? You must be really hurt after everything you've been through with your mama and now Landon too."

I started tearing up.

"I'm so sorry, Milah Jo. I had no right to treat you the way I have the past few weeks. I just couldn't bring myself to talk to anyone. How stupid am I?"

We had reached the school parking lot and had just gotten out of the car. Milah Jo wrapped me into a big bear hug and told me, "Jane, you're not alone anymore. You can always trust me to be there for you. Promise me you'll never suffer through anything like this alone again."

I was sobbing and hugging her back as tightly as I could.

"I promise, Milah Jo, I promise."

She let go of me and said, "Okay, well now we've got to get you cleaned up so we can get inside this stupid farm school before the tardy bell rings."

And that's what she did. Milah Jo took me straight to the restrooms and ran everybody out of there so she could make me presentable. Our day was pretty well split except for lunch. We still always sat at our table in the back corner. We hadn't been sitting there long when Landon set his tray down on the table just as he had done that first time he had sat with us at lunch.

"May I sit with you ladies today?" he asked.

I couldn't even look up at him.

"I'm not so sure that's a good idea, Landon," I said.

He put my chin in his hand and turned my face toward his.

"Jane, I really miss you. Please."

The touch of his hand on my face sent a flutter through my stomach. I had to admit that as mad as I was at him, I missed him desperately. I really wanted him to sit with us, but my pride wouldn't let me say yes.

"You made your choice, Landon. Go sit with Kyle."

He let go of my chin.

"Please, Jane."

I just turned my head away from him and started eating my pizza. Landon walked off and went over to sit with Kyle. Milah Jo didn't say one word to him. That was unbelievable, because nothing kept that girl quiet. She didn't stay quiet long, though.

Milah Jo looked over Landon's way and then looked at me.

"Girl, that boy looked like his dog had done died," she said. "I know he hurt you, but maybe he wants to make it up to you."

I looked right back at her.

"Milah Jo, I don't think he *can* make it up to me. He's broken my heart. I've lived the last four years of my life miserable because of someone else's drug use. I can't do it all over again."

Was she really suggesting I give Landon another chance after everything that had happened?

"Are you saying I should let him try to make it up to me?" I asked. "Why would I set myself up to be hurt like that again? I know how this ends, Milah Jo, and it isn't good!"

A serious look I'd never seen before came across Milah Jo's face. Milah Jo was not often serious about anything.

"Jane, I know your mama hurt ya real bad when she messed up a second time, but Landon is not her. I believe everyone deserves a second chance and I don't understand why you won't let him try. Look at that boy; he is absolutely gorgeous and crazy about you. Maybe the pills aren't a problem; maybe he's just taking them every now and then."

Everything she was telling me I'd already gone over and over in my mind. I'd done nothing but think of Landon over the past few weeks. I'd thought about how hurt I'd been to find out he was doing drugs. I'd thought about the first time he'd touched me in the basement and how it had sent a shock right through me. I'd thought about when we'd spent the night in that nasty tent and how he'd held me all night. I'd also thought a lot about how I couldn't see living the rest of my life without him. I got that sick feeling in the pit of my stomach just thinking about it. I guess all that thinking had left me with quite the decision. It was a decision I didn't know how to make.

I couldn't decide to live without him and I couldn't decide to live with the dope either. But I had to choose one. I had given Landon an ultimatum, yet there I sat with one of my own. How was that fair? I hadn't done anything wrong—why should I make the sacrifices? He'd chosen the pills, and the only way I could choose him was to choose the pills too. That went against everything I believed in, but I was actually considering going through with it. I wanted Landon in my life. I wanted him to be a part of me. I wanted to be a part of him. When you love someone, aren't you supposed to take the bad with the good? Aren't you supposed to love them unconditionally and accept them for who they are?

Support them when they need help and not desert them?

I missed him. I did want to support Landon. I wanted to be there for him. I didn't want anything to happen to him. Didn't he need me there to watch over him and make sure he was okay?

Milah Jo smacked me on the arm.

"Earth to Jane. The lunch bell rang. We gotta get to class, hon."

I snapped out of my thoughts.

"Oh, okay. Sorry. I was just thinking."

"Ya reckon? I could see the smoke comin' outta your ears," Milah Jo said, chuckling.

"Speaking of smoke, Milah Jo, you stink. Were you smoking in the girls' restroom again?" I teased her.

We went our separate ways to class. I couldn't concentrate on anything for the rest of the day. I just kept thinking about Landon and rationalizing why I should stay with him. I didn't know how it would work. I had so much pent-up frustration with Mother and her drug use. I despised drugs like most people despised child molesters. That was the truth—I hated that shit. How could I love Landon if I despised what he did? Ugh! More questions I didn't know the answers to. I kept asking myself question after question, but I couldn't seem to come up with an answer. I thought I was going to give myself a migraine.

When the last bell rang for the day, I headed toward the parking lot to catch up with Milah Jo. I saw Landon standing by his car like he was waiting on someone. Oh, man. I could not deal with another run-in with him. When I got to Milah Jo's car, it was locked. She'd insisted on locking it even after I'd assured her no one would dare try to steal it. She'd flipped me off and locked it anyway. I couldn't get in, so I had to stand there by the car and wait for her. I really didn't want to give Landon any more time than he already had to approach me. Yet I found myself standing there looking over at him every few seconds. I really did miss him. It was so hard to see him every day and not talk to him, touch him, or kiss him. Before all this had happened, the only place I ever wanted to be was in his arms. That was still where I wanted to be.

I saw Milah Jo come out the gym doors. Geez, finally! I wondered what had taken her so long. I looked back over at Landon to make sure he wasn't coming my way. Instead, he was standing by his car, and Ivy Lang was walking right toward him. What the hell was she doing here? I'd thought there were rules against non-students being on school grounds. Better yet, why was she here to see Landon? I'd thought she was Kyle's friend. As if I didn't have enough to deal with, now I had to deal with this. I knew I was gawking, but I couldn't bring myself to look away. Ivy went up to Landon, gave him a hug, and got into the front seat of his car.

Milah Jo came up behind me and scared the crap out of me. She put her arm around me.

"Oh, no, she didn't! Who the hell is that?" she scoffed.

I wiggled myself out of her arm. I couldn't handle anybody touching me right now.

"That's Ivy Lang," I told her. "Did I forget to mention her when I told you about everything?"

Milah Jo gave me a very sarcastic look.

"Uh, yeah, I think I would have remembered that part," she snarked. "What's up with a name like Ivy Lang? It sounds like a stripper or porn star name."

"Did you see her?" I mumbled.

Milah Jo unlocked my door and went around the car to unlock hers.

"Yes, I saw her," she said. "I didn't know which part was going to fall out of her clothes first, her ass or her boobs."

I watched Landon get into the driver's seat of his car. I was really hoping Kyle would join them so I could understand why Ivy would be getting into Landon's car. But he didn't. It was just Landon and Ivy. As I was getting into Milah Jo's car, I was thinking how things just couldn't possibly get any worse, when Emily came walking past the car.

"Well, it looks like it didn't take him long to get over you," she said. "He gets bored pretty quick, you know. I can't believe you two lasted as long as you did. What was he thinking fraternizing with the bastard offspring of the hired help?"

Milah Jo interrupted: "Don't pay any attention to her, Jane. She's just a miserable little girl who gets off on downgrading people."

Emily laughed.

"Nice car, Milah Jo. The roach mobile suits you well. It totally makes sense that only trash would ride in it."

Emily started walking toward her new SUV. She sure did have a way of bringing people down. I really wished I wouldn't let her get to me, and I really wished Milah Jo wouldn't let her get to her either. But before I could do anything to stop it, Milah Jo had Emily by the hair on the back of her head. I tried to break them up, but Milah Jo wouldn't let go. She got in quite a few good punches before Mr. McDonald broke it up. We all three ended up in Principal Ferguson's office. I guess it looked as though I was in on it, too, when Mr. McDonald saw us. Milah Jo tried to explain to Principal Ferguson that I was trying to pull her off Emily, but he wouldn't hear it. Emily had told him we both had ganged up on her, and that was what he believed.

That was just what I needed. A ten-day suspension, a court date, and Mother and Mrs. Whitman called to come to the school at the same time. Mrs. Whitman was not going to be happy with me. She didn't like me anyway, and now she would think I'd thumped on her precious Emily. Mother arrived with Lizzie in tow right after Mrs. Whitman had come in. We were all sitting in the hall. Principal Ferguson had given us our what-for and sent us to the lobby to wait on our parents. Mother sat down next to me.

"What the hell happened, Jane?" she asked.

I tried to explain to her how things had really gone down, but Emily overheard us and butted in.

"Clara, your daughter is a menace. You should put her back in foster care. Look what she did to my face," Emily whined.

She was interrupted by Principal Ferguson. He told us all to come into his office. He started to tell our mothers what had happened when there was a knock on the door. It was Ms. Flowers, the secretary, letting the principal know Milah Jo's grandmother had arrived. The secretary escorted her in and Principal Ferguson started his version of the incident all over again. Milah Jo kept butting in to tell them I'd had nothing to do with it. Principal Ferguson was explaining the negative consequences of fighting on school property when Ms. Flowers knocked on the door again. She announced that a witness had come forth. When I turned around to see who it was, I heard Emily shout, "Landon!"

Landon explained to our parents and Principal Ferguson what he had seen from his car. Emily might have thought she had pull in this school, but Landon had her beat. That boy was the golden child of Whitman High School. Of course, they believed everything he told them, even though Emily tried to talk her way out of her lie by saying the punches were coming so fast she thought for sure I had made some of them.

So, Landon had saved the day. Big whoop-de-do! Should we give him a medal for telling the truth? No, I didn't think so. All and all, though, I was really glad I wasn't in trouble. Landon, Mother, and I were all excused to go home. I didn't get an apology or anything from Principal Ferguson. When we got outside, Landon asked Mother if she minded if he speak to me for a few minutes. Well, crap! After everything, he was going to get his five minutes anyway.

"Jane, will you ride home with me so we can talk?" he asked.

Those big brown eyes were trying their best to sink into my soul. How could I say no to him, yet how could I go with him?

I looked down at the ground.

"I can't, Landon," I said. "I'm sure Mother won't let me. I would say she's pretty ticked that she had to come down here."

Of course, Mother had to butt in.

"Jane, I have a few errands to run, so you go ahead and ride home with Landon. I know you don't like going to the grocery store anyway."

Mother and Lizzie walked off without waiting for my reply. I guess that meant I was riding home with Landon whether I agreed to it or not.

"Great! Let's go," I snapped at him.

Landon didn't say anything. He just started walking toward his car and I followed, stomping my little feet all the way. As soon as I sat down in the passenger seat, I had to ask.

"So, where did Ivy go? I saw her over here with you earlier."

Landon frowned at me.

"She left with Kyle."

I turned to look out the window.

"Oh."

Landon reached over and grabbed my hand, but I pulled it away from him.

"Jane, would you please let me talk to you without giving me all the attitude?" Landon asked. "I'm so sorry for everything I said and did to you. I didn't mean to scare you that day, and I sure didn't mean to say the things to you that I did. I miss you so much and I know you miss me too. I can feel it. I know every time you glance my way. Our souls are bound together, Jane. Please don't let this come between us. Nothing should be able to come between our love."

I finally turned toward him. Tears were streaming down my face. I knew he was right. Our souls had been bound together. Being without him had been horrible, and I really didn't know how much longer I was going to be able to make it without him.

"How, Landon? How is it possible for us to be together while you continue to get high? I don't know how I can deal with that," I told him.

I think he knew he was getting through to me, because he gave me a small piece of that amazing smile.

"I don't do it that often, Jane," he assured me. "When I do, it's not that much, and I promise I'll never do it in front of you or around you. I need you."

This was crazy. How could I even be considering this? I knew this couldn't end well, yet I couldn't stand the thought of not being with him. The last few weeks had been hell without him. I loved him so much. Maybe I could eventually convince him to quit. Wouldn't it be better if I were with him to make sure he was okay?

"Landon, can you promise me that you won't do anything dangerous and that you'll do your best to quit?" I asked.

Landon reached over and slid his hand on the back of my neck.

"Jane, I can't guarantee that I'm going to quit, but I really don't do it that often, so you have nothing to worry about," he told me. "I won't hide anything from you anymore. I promise."

I sighed.

"Landon, you say you won't hide anything anymore. But you will. You won't want me to worry, or you won't want me to be disappointed, and you'll hide things from me. Don't make promises you can't keep."

Landon pulled my face close to his.

"Jane, I promise I will not do anything to worry or upset you. You mean too much to me. I don't want to risk losing you again."

The tears were now pouring down my face.

"What do you mean losing me *again*?" I asked. "What makes you think you have me back?"

Landon now had my face in his hands. He rested his forehead against mine.

"Because you're letting me touch you again," he answered. "It's killed me that I haven't been able to touch you the past few weeks."

He kissed me. I couldn't fight it, so I kissed him back. I'd missed the touch of his warm lips so much that I didn't have the strength to fight against something I wanted anyway.

I didn't know how this was going to work, but I was willing to give it a try.

What was I thinking?

The next few weeks were strange, but at the same time, it was nice to be back in Landon's arms again. I'd missed him so much that I was willing to go against everything I believed in to be with him. Our relationship still wasn't the same as it had been, though. I worried about him all the time. I hovered a good bit. I was questioning in my mind everything that he did. I often wondered who he was with and what he was doing. He got tons of text messages, and it drove me crazy that I had no idea what he was talking about in them. It was like I'd become obsessed with his every move. I'd lost myself somehow and consumed myself with him. I was codependent. I was sure of it. His addiction had become my problem too.

I definitely hadn't thought everything through when I'd agreed to keep seeing Landon even though he would not agree to give up the freaking pills. *What the hell had I been thinking?* I should have known this was going to be what it would be like. I worried about him all the time. I was sure he'd lost another five pounds. He'd promised me everything would be out in the open, but I constantly had this aching feeling that something was going on that I didn't know about. He thought I was paranoid, of course.

I might have been bordering on stalking him, and I was starting to annoy him. Landon got tired of me griping at him about his weight all the time. I was pretty sure he'd turned into a vampire because the boy never slept except for when we were sitting on the couch having a conversation or watching a movie. He nodded out pretty quickly then, and it annoyed the shit out of me. It reminded me of Mother's dope days.

I got so angry at Landon. I'd read that anger is a secondary emotion, so I figured I was angry because I was hurt. I was hurt that he wouldn't stop using. He claimed he didn't use that much, but I didn't believe that. Things wouldn't have been getting so bad if he were getting high only every now and then. He spent way too much time with Kyle for me to believe that.

I was so tired of my mood revolving around Landon's. I walked on eggshells around him most of the time. My toes were getting tired, but I couldn't seem to convince them to walk away. I loved Landon too much to leave him like this. There had to be a way for me to help him.

It had gotten to the point that I could tell when he was not using. When he was not sleeping or sick, he was a complete dick. He'd gotten ticked off at me on the way home from school one day and decided to drive like a maniac. He terrified me. I knew he was in a bad mood because he wasn't high. How was it fair that I ended up in these situations? I must have been some kind of opiate-addict magnet. Just call me "Opiate Jane." I would have thought with a name like mine I would have attracted potheads. But no, I loved people who seemed determined to kill themselves slowly with opiates. It was so hard to watch someone I loved die a little every day and know there wasn't anything I could do to stop it.

I had seen Landon pull out of the garage at about two in the morning several times over the past few weeks. Things were supposed to be getting better, not worse. I didn't get why his parents didn't say anything to him about running around all hours of the night. When I asked him where he was going, he would just tell me he had to run to town. When I asked why, he would throw me that beautiful smile and change the conversation. I was pretty sure he had this theory that he wasn't lying if he told me only part of the truth. I didn't think he realized that the silent lies were usually the worst ones.

I decided that one of these nights I was going to hide out in his car just to see where he went. So help me if he was meeting up with Ivy! I would go ballistic on them both. That was one promise he'd made to me: that he would have nothing more to do with her. He didn't understand why I was making a big deal out of it, because to him she was just a connection. But who the hell would want their boyfriend meeting up with a chick who looked like she'd just climbed down off her pole? I had to admit, though, that was not the only reason I didn't want him around her. I didn't like that she knew about me and I didn't know about her, and I really couldn't handle the fact that they were part of this whole other drug world that I was not part of. It made me feel like the outcast. How sad was that? I was jealous of the relationship between the junkie and the drug dealer. When I was griping to Landon about using the pills, he had Ivy to talk to. And since she did them too, she could comfort him. I couldn't stand it.

I was officially driving myself crazy. Every time Landon left, every time his phone rang, and every time he got a text, my mind started wondering if it was Ivy. You would have thought they'd had an affair. When he left in the middle of the night it was the worst, but the constant texting was running a close second. I would have loved to have gotten ahold of that freaking phone.

I sounded like a crazed lunatic! I probably would have been considered a stalker if I weren't already Landon's girlfriend. As much as I would have liked to put a lot of the blame on Ivy,

I knew deep down inside it was the pills that were driving me crazy. How could those stupid little inanimate objects be more important to him than I was? I didn't understand why he wanted to risk everything we had just so he could get high. It really made me feel like I wasn't enough for him.

I didn't think I was enough for anyone. I wasn't enough for my mother not to want the drugs, and I wasn't enough for my father to even consider sticking around. I knew I had issues. I thought maybe I should see a shrink, but I was sure a shrink would have just put me on meds to make me feel better. Then I would have been no better off than any of the people who were supposed to love me. I would never do anything like that even if it were a legitimate prescription. I wanted to make sure Lizzie always had one person in this world she could count on.

Society pretty much revolves around drugs now. Doctors hand out meds like candy, and usually the government pays for it. Even at only sixteen years old, I'd seen enough to know things were messed up. Why couldn't things just be normal? When would I get my normal? What was normal anyway? If someone had asked me what that normal was that I wanted, I probably couldn't have told them. I'd never had normal. Normal, to me, probably would have been to live in a world where the people I loved didn't do drugs.

One night, Landon and I were supposed to go out. He'd promised me a night out without any of his so-called buddies around. We were going out to dinner and then to a movie, and I was looking forward to it. No matter how much I dwelled on everything that was wrong with our relationship, I craved the things that were good about it. I guess that kind of made me a junkie too, craving something I knew wasn't good for me and that could end up hurting me in the long run. Yep, that sounded familiar, but I couldn't help myself. Every time that boy put his arms around me, I felt like I was finally home. It had been a long time since I'd felt like anywhere was home. I just was not ready to give that up. It felt so freaking good. Landon was the first person I'd ever looked in the eye and seen my own reflection looking back. He saw me for me and loved me. He knew I was flawed and broken and loved me anyway. Yet, I saw him for who he was and I judged him for it. Ugh! Why did this have to be so hard? Just once, couldn't something be easy?

So there I was, getting ready for a date with Landon even though just an hour ago I'd been questioning my relationship with him—and questioning my sanity. It was no wonder I was so conflicted. I had no idea what to do. I knew what I needed and I knew what I wanted, and those things weren't the same. I wanted Landon sober. But Landon didn't want that, so where did that leave me? It left me hanging on to any shred of good in our relationship, knowing that at some point it would end. That was a sad feeling, and I tended to push it back and stay in denial.

I kept hoping things would get better. They'd been pretty good at first after we'd gotten back together. It had seemed like Landon was relieved to not have to hide it anymore. He'd been so open about everything with me. But then it started to feel like he was trying to be sneaky sometimes. I just didn't know what to do.

Landon knocked on the door right at 6 p.m. Lizzie ran to the door, declaring she would get it. She'd adored Landon ever since he'd taken her to see the jellyfish at Mineral Springs. Mother just gave us looks, and I knew it was because Mrs. Whitman did not approve. I knew Mother was worried that my relationship might cost her her job.

I hurried out the door and Landon followed. We got into his

car without saying anything to each other and headed out the driveway. We were almost into Mount Orab before either of us spoke. Landon placed his hand on my leg and gave it a little squeeze.

"What's wrong with my girl tonight? Why are you so quiet?" he asked.

I gave him one of those frown-smiles my mother always said I was famous for.

"I've just been thinking a lot today. I have a lot on my mind, you know."

Landon put his hand back on the steering wheel.

"Really, Jane, are you going to start this already? I thought you were looking forward to tonight and it being just the two of us. Why would you want to ruin it before we even get started? Tonight is supposed to be fun."

Of course he was going to blame this on me. I folded my arms and huffed.

"I'm not trying to ruin the night, Landon Whitman," I said. "You shouldn't ask questions you don't want the answers to. You know the reason I'm upset. It's the reason I'm upset 98 percent of the time. I just don't know how you think we can go out and pretend like everything is okay, when obviously it's not. I can't do it anymore. You're going to have to start looking at things from my perspective."

Landon shot me a nasty look. He pulled off the road into a gas station and parked the car.

"Damn it, Jane, your perspective is blurred," he argued. "You see everything jaded thanks to your mother. I'm not like her. I don't do the shit she did. What I do, I only do every now and then, and it's not even that strong. Your mother was a heroin addict.

That's a lot different from popping a pill once in a while. I'm sure I could stop using them without even getting dope-sick."

I could feel the tears welling up in my eyes.

"Then why don't you try, Landon?"

He laughed at me.

"Because I don't want to try, Jane. I don't have to."

Now the tears were running down my cheeks. I turned to look out the window so he couldn't see I was crying.

"You don't want to stop, Landon, because you know you *will* be dope-sick. Tell me, how often is once in a while?"

These conversations were usually done via text, but for some reason today it was face to face. He always avoided answering my questions when we were texting. Now, I had him stuck in this car with me and he was going to give me some answers.

He shrugged his shoulders.

"I don't know—one or two times a month maybe."

Crying or not, I didn't care. I turned to face Landon.

"You would sit here and lie right to my face? I've counted five times in the last week that I've seen the remnants of a pill in your nose. How am I to believe a word you say if you can't be honest with me, Landon? Why can't you see what you're doing to yourself? I bet you're lucky to weigh 140 pounds, and honestly, Landon, when was the last time you washed your hair or shaved?"

He cocked his jaw sideways. I knew I'd hit a nerve.

"Jane, I've told you a hundred freaking times: I weigh a buck sixty. I'm so sick of you ragging on my weight all the time, and now you're telling me I don't shower enough? Go ahead and get the rest of your griping out too. Let's see: I text too much, I don't spend enough time with you, you think I've been talking to Ivy, and you want to know what it is I do at night. You're always making accusations, Jane. Why can't you just let things be and enjoy yourself?"

I just turned my head. I didn't want to hear how it was all my fault anymore. The rest of the night was ruined. We went to dinner and watched the movie in silence.

Stowaway

Landon hadn't answered my phone calls all day. I finally went over to his house around five because I couldn't stand it anymore. Mrs. Whitman said Landon had been in bed all day and she was pretty sure he was coming down with something. She wouldn't let me in to see him. My mother had the day off, so she couldn't tell me anything either. I finally decided to lie down around midnight. I was really worried about Landon. I couldn't sleep. What if he took too much of something and nobody realized it until it was too late?

At around 12:30 a.m., I saw his bedroom light come on. I texted him to see what was up. He texted me back that he hadn't been feeling well and he thought he was coming down with the flu. I asked him if there was anything I could do. I guess he must have been texting with somebody else at the same time he was texting me, because he sent me a text that said he would be in town in twenty minutes. What the hell? I thought he was sick. I decided it was time I found out why he went to "town" in the middle of the night. I guess I already knew why, but I wanted to know where. I wanted to know every person who was contributing to killing my Landon. I wanted to find out who they were and confront them all. It didn't matter to me that they were drug dealers. I didn't care if I could get hurt. I just wanted them to stop supplying Landon with that stuff.

I got out of bed, got dressed, and quietly snuck out the front door. I went into the garage, climbed into the back of Landon's

Mustang, and got down onto the floor. He had a jacket in the back seat, so I put it over my head. I was pretty sure he wouldn't notice me, but I was really starting to shake. What in the world would he say if he found me back there?

He got into the car not long after I got in. I was really freaking out! We were about fifteen minutes into the drive before he parked the car. I waited for about five minutes after Landon got out before I peeked my head up to see where we were. We were at his uncle's house, the same place where we'd played paintball. Why would he have sent that text saying he was going to town? It had to be some kind of dope code.

I climbed into the front seat and quietly got out of the car. I wanted a closer look at what was going on. I snuck over to the side of the house and peeked into the corner of one of the lit-up windows. The window had a crack in it so I could partially hear what they were saying inside. Landon was talking to an older guy who must have been his uncle. He was begging his uncle for another chance. His uncle started scolding him over some money Landon had already cost him. Landon sat down in a chair across from his uncle with the most awful look I'd ever seen on his face.

"I'm sick, Uncle Mac," Landon moaned. "I just need a couple to get me through school tomorrow. I promise I'll replace your money. I've got to have something. I'm sick."

Landon did look bad. His face was pale, he looked like he'd lost another five pounds since I'd seen him last, and he was holding on to his stomach as if it were killing him. Evidently the flu wasn't the culprit, though. Landon was dope-sick. He'd been telling me this whole time that he only did drugs every now and then. He'd been lying to me. He'd been doing them pretty frequently if he was dope-sick.

I didn't understand how in the world he could owe anybody money. That boy was loaded! I heard his uncle say something about how he wasn't "giving in this time," that he was going to have to start treating Landon like every other junkie instead of like family. He flat-out refused to give Landon anything.

A woman walked into the room and ran her hand through Landon's hair as if he were a puppy.

"Oh, Mac, look at the poor boy," she said. "Maybe you should help him out this one last time."

She looked really familiar, but I knew I'd never met her. Why did she look so familiar?

Mac stood and yelled at the woman.

"Lily, I will not give him any more handouts! That boy's family has more money in their little fingers than we will ever see in a lifetime. I know he can find a way to pay me what he owes me. He'll figure it out. No more fronts."

I decided I'd better head back to the car. Landon would probably be leaving soon, since he couldn't get what he'd come for. Right as I crouched down to get past the windows, I heard a noise in the bushes behind me. I figured it was a dog or something and shrugged it off as I went toward the car. But someone grabbed my arm as soon as I got to the corner of the house. It scared me to death. It was an older man with long gray hair. He looked like something right out of the mountains. He turned me toward him and got in my face.

"What the hell do you think you're doing, young lady?" he asked.

I froze; I didn't know what to say. I didn't want to tell him I was with Landon and get Landon in more trouble with his uncle.

"Ain't got no answer, huh? That's all right. I'll take you in the house to see Mac. He can deal with you," he grunted.

He dragged me by the arm around the corner of the house and in through the back door. When Landon saw me come in, his mouth dropped.

"Hey, Mac, look what I found outside peeking in the window. What do you suppose I do with this?"

The gray-haired man let go of my arm and gave me a shove toward Landon's uncle.

Mac jumped up out of his chair, grabbed a pocket knife off the table, and headed toward me. Landon ran over in front of me and stopped his uncle.

"She's with me, Uncle Mac," Landon said. "She was supposed to stay in the car."

Landon turned and gave me a furious look, and Mac backed off.

"What the hell are you doing, Landon? Trying to get me busted? I can't be having this shit. I've told you time and time again not to bring anybody but Kyle with you. I thought you were smarter than that, boy."

Landon put his hands up in the air.

"I know, I know. It's pretty dark outside. I thought she would stay in the car and you would never have known she was here. I'm sorry, Uncle Mac. It won't happen again. I swear."

Mac sat back down in his chair.

"I'm glad to hear you're sorry, boy, but I just can't let her leave. She saw too much. She could run straight to the cops."

Landon shook his head.

"She wouldn't do that Uncle Mac," he said. "She knows better."

Mac's face was getting redder by the minute.

"How am I supposed to believe that, boy? You thought she was smart enough to stay in the car and Jed caught her snooping in the window. I can't take that chance. Jed, put her in the back room and make sure she can't get out. I need time to think about what it is I'm going to do with her."

I couldn't help myself. I opened my big fat mouth before I realized what I was doing.

"Wait! Don't worry, Mac," I said. "I'll keep your secret and make you a deal. I won't tell anybody anything about your operation here if you promise to not give your nephew any more of that crap. I can't believe his own family would contribute to killing him just so they could make a buck."

Mac threw his hands into the air.

"Jed, get her and put her in the other room before she makes me mad enough to kill her. Get her the hell out of my sight. Now!"

Jed grabbed me by the arm again.

"Sure thing, boss."

Landon came over and knocked Jed's hand away from my arm. Mac moved quickly over to where we were and grabbed hold of Landon. Mac was a big guy, and Landon didn't stand a chance against him. Jed told Lily to get him some rope as he dragged me into the hall.

Landon tried to follow, but Mac still had a hold of him.

"You're going to stay right here with me, boy. We're going to have a talk," Mac scolded.

Jed took me to the back of the house. It was really dark and I had no idea what he was going to do with me. He took me into an empty room and Lily followed. Jed told me to sit down and Lily handed him the rope. Jed tied my hands together, then my feet, and then my arms to my legs. I was pretty sure it wasn't the first time he'd tied someone up. He seemed to know what he was doing. I was terrified. I should have kept my mouth shut. I should have kept my butt in the car. This was not a world I wanted to be a part of, yet there I sat, tied up in the middle of it. They left me in the room by myself, and it sounded as if they'd locked the door on their way out. I didn't know how I was going to get out of this, and I had no idea what they were out there doing to Landon. I was so scared that I'd started to cry. I should have stayed home. Thanks to my curiosity, I now had Landon and myself in a world of trouble. Any sane person knows you don't piss off dope dealers. This was crazy. What the hell had I been thinking?

I sat in the room for at least a good hour. I could hear movement in the other room, but I couldn't hear well enough to figure out what was going on. I was so worried about Landon. I had tried to wiggle myself out of the ropes, but it was no use. Jed had tied them really tight. It wasn't long after I'd given up on trying to get out of the ropes when I heard a really loud noise. It scared me. I didn't know if it was some kind of explosion or if it was a gun shot. I started screaming for Landon.

There was a crack in the window and a strange smell was coming in through it. I heard the noise again. The second time, I was sure it was an explosion of some kind. It sounded a lot like one of those really big fireworks they let off on the Fourth of July. The smell was getting really bad. I had to get out of here. I didn't know if the explosion had happened outside or if it had happened in the house and had caught the house on fire. I was moving around a lot trying to get loose when Landon burst through the door. He didn't even waste time to untie me. He just picked me up and carried me out into the hallway.

The smell was starting to get to me; I felt like I was choking. When I finally stopped coughing, I asked Landon what had happened. He just shook his head and told me not to talk. Once we made it to the front porch, he sat me down and untied me.

I was so out of breath.

"Landon, what is going on? What was that noise and what is that smell?"

Landon was frantically untying me.

"There was an explosion in the shed. Everybody ran out there when it happened. They're busy dealing with it right now, but we've got to get the hell out of here before they realize they left us alone in the house."

Landon finished untying me, grabbed my arm, turned me around, and pointed me toward the car. When we got out into the yard, I noticed there were three people standing at the corner of the house. I stopped to take a second look when I realized one of them was Ivy Lang. Then it dawned on me that the woman in the house reminded me of Ivy and that was why she'd looked so familiar. They were sisters. That must have been who Landon had been texting. I knew that girl was bad news. Now it all made sense. Landon had said his uncle's girlfriend and her sister lived here. Ivy lived here.

Landon came back to where I was standing and dragged me to the car.

"What the hell are you doing, Jane? We've got to get out of here. If Mac and his gang don't get us, the cops will. After an explosion like that, they have to be on their way. We've got to go *now*."

Landon was quiet until we got out onto the main road. I could tell he was scared and upset. He was gripping the steering wheel so tight his knuckles were snow white. Finally he spoke.

"Jane, what were you doing? Do you realize he really could have—and would have—killed you? The only thing that saved your life was that damn explosion. How did you know where I was? How did you even get here?"

I tucked my knees up to my chest and wrapped my arms around my legs.

"I snuck into the back of your car before you left," I said. "I wanted to see where it is that you go in the middle of the night. Once we were here, I couldn't help myself. I had to take a look inside. I wanted to see what you were doing. I guess I should have known."

Landon pressed his foot down harder on the accelerator. The speedometer read 85 mph.

"Oh, here we go," he said sarcastically. "You should have known what? That I was going after pills? Yes, I was. But only because I'm not feeling well and I knew they would make feel better. I'm catching the flu or something."

I slammed my legs onto the floor of the car.

"After all the crap we've been through tonight, don't even give me that bullshit, Landon!" I yelled. "I know you're freaking dope-sick. Why can't you just admit it? You own up to doing them, but you just can't seem to own up to how much control they have over you. That stuff is running your life. You live for it anymore. If you're not high, you're chasing it or sick because you can't find it. Do you think I'm stupid, Landon? I know you're high when you're in a great mood. I see the white stuff crusted in your nose sometimes. I know what that is. I know that when you're impatient, quick-tempered, or not feeling well, that means you're out of them. You must have forgotten that I've lived through all this stuff a time or two. I've seen it before."

Landon still had a very tight grip on the steering wheel and was still flying down the road. He was really scaring me. I had never seen him like this.

"Why do you put up with my pathetic ass if you know everything then?"

Why *did* I put up with all this? I didn't let my mother get away with any of it. I still gave her a hard time about it, yet there I was sitting with Landon after almost having my throat slashed by his drug dealer uncle. What was wrong with me? Oh, right: I loved him. That's what was wrong with me. I'd always heard stories about women who had been beaten by their boyfriend or husband. People would ask them why they stayed with someone who hurt them and they'd always say, "Because I love him." That's how idiotic I sounded. *Why do you stay, Jane?* Because I love him. Ugh!

"Because I love you, Landon Whitman. That's why," I cried.

That was the first time I'd ever said the actual words to Landon. He stayed silent. He did manage to slow down the car for the rest of the ride home. He parked the car in the garage. I got out and walked around to the driver's side.

"Aren't you going to get out of the car?" I asked.

Landon laid his seat back.

"Nope, this is where I'll be staying tonight."

I wrinkled my eyebrows.

"Why would you want to sleep in your car? You have a perfectly good bed up in your room."

He shrugged his shoulders.

"Just makes things easier that way."

I was getting frustrated. Just answer the freaking question; don't dance around it.

"It makes what easier?" I persisted.

He rested his head back against the seat and closed his eyes.

"Just go to bed, Jane."

I started walking toward the garage door. He could be such an ass sometimes. As mad as I was at him, I couldn't stand the thought of leaving him there by himself, sick. I turned around and climbed back into the passenger seat of the car.

Landon turned his head slightly my way and didn't even open his eyes.

"What are you doing?" he asked.

I folded my arms across my chest.

"I'm staying in the car too then."

He turned his head back toward the window and mumbled, "Whatever."

It didn't seem like it took him very long to fall asleep. So there I sat, in his car, watching him sleep. He hadn't been asleep for long when he started moving around a lot. His legs started kicking around. Then his arms started to twitch. He couldn't stay still. I don't know how he was sleeping the way he was moving around. He would try to pull his legs up to him, but the steering wheel kept getting in the way. This was so much worse than I'd thought. He must have been using a lot more than he said he was.

I sat there for a while just watching him. I knew I shouldn't snoop through his stuff, but for some reason I felt like I had to. I knew I was going to find things I didn't want to, but I had to look anyway. I slid his phone out of his coat pocket and started searching his texts. The first one I read was from Ivy. She was telling him to come over and she would hook him up. I hated that girl. There were multiple texts from her, and they were all drug-related. I really didn't think anything physical was going on between them, but the constant contact between the two of them drove me crazy. I'd asked him multiple times to not have anything to do with her, but he continued to do it anyway. He'd told me he didn't talk to her anymore, but apparently he just couldn't help himself. The drugs had taken him over and she was a way for him to get them.

There were lots of other texts from people I didn't know. I would say 97 percent of the 269 texts in his phone were about drugs. The other 3 percent were from me. I didn't even bother to read his sent messages. I was nervous he would wake up and catch me with his phone, so I slid it back into his pocket.

I rested my head against the seat and closed my eyes for a few minutes. I was getting really tired. It was going on 4 a.m. I'd been through a really stressful night and it had exhausted me. I would have to head into the house soon. I didn't want Mother to realize I was gone. I sat upright; I didn't want to fall asleep. I decided to open the glove box and see what was inside, and I pulled out a small tin box and opened it. I shouldn't have been shocked, but I was. I couldn't believe Landon would be so careless to carry something like that right in his car. The tin box had a small piece of paper in it. It also had a small straw and white powdery residue all over the inside. He was taking a huge risk with this, which meant he was completely out of control. What was I supposed to do? Something horrible was going to happen to Landon if he didn't stop. He *had* to stop.

I had just put the tin box back into the glove box when I heard Landon's voice.

"Why are you still out here? You need to go before you get into trouble."

"I was watching you sleep," I replied, "if that's what you call sleeping. You kicked and twitched all over the place. How long has it been since you had anything? I didn't realize things were this bad. My feelings for you seem to have blinded me from the truth.

I should have seen what was right in front of my face. Landon, you're killing yourself. I'm so afraid for you. This needs to stop. Please, Landon, stop."

He frowned at me.

"Jane, I'm fine," he insisted. "I have everything under control. I'm not going to discuss this with you. I'm going to hang out here for a few and then head in. You need to get to bed before your mother figures out you're gone. I'll see you tomorrow."

I sat there for a few minutes. I was beginning to wonder why I even tried. I decided I was very tired and I really didn't want to get into trouble. I got out of the car, slammed the door, and walked out of the garage without giving Landon a second look. I snuck back into my room, threw on some pajamas, and climbed into bed. I'd been lying there for about ten minutes when I heard Landon's Mustang pull out of the driveway. I looked out the window and watched him drive away. He must have been on the hunt again.

It's so sad how addiction takes over a wonderful person and turns them into someone who will lie or steal to get their next high.

Every time Landon left, I worried he wouldn't make it back. I was so upset, I figured I wouldn't be able to sleep. Being tired must have overruled being upset, though, because it wasn't long before I fell asleep. I dreamed of Landon's funeral. It made realize I would have to do something soon or that nightmare would become a reality.

Enough

After everything that had happened the night before, I woke up with the realization that I'd had enough. It was a realization I'd come to way too many times before but had never had the guts to act on. Almost getting myself killed might have had something to do with me having the guts finally.

Why was it that even though I knew what was right and what should be done, it was such a struggle to do it? How was I supposed to walk away from someone I loved so much? Didn't that make me selfish to leave him all alone when he needed me so much? Because no matter how much I told myself it was for his own good, I knew I was doing this for me—for my sanity.

I'd tried to accept Landon for who he was, but I couldn't do it. I couldn't sit by and watch him kill himself, because I knew that was what he was doing. He was doing it slowly, and it was like I was giving him the okay to die. I was watching him wither away in front of my eyes. I didn't understand why I was the only one who saw it. Why didn't his family and friends see it too? I knew why Kyle didn't see it. He was too far gone into the drugs himself to care about anybody else.

Landon had lost weight, his cheeks were sunken in, he nodded off in the middle of conversations, and he rarely shaved anymore. It was like he just didn't care. He was out all hours of the night and didn't sleep much at all unless, of course, he was mid-conversation.

I was so angry at him for doing this to himself and for making me go through it too. I loved him so much, and the last thing I wanted to do was let him go. What would happen to him if I weren't there to watch him? But what good was I doing watching him die? I was so conflicted. I didn't know what to do. I wanted Landon, but I didn't want the life he was living. I wanted a normal relationship, one in which I didn't have to worry about walking into a room and finding him dead; or watch him withdraw all night long, kicking his legs all over the place in his sleep; or wonder if he were sitting in jail or the morgue because he wasn't home at two in the morning. Confused or not, I knew what I needed to do. I had to give him an ultimatum again. But that was like the worst word ever to use with an addict. Addicts don't like to be told what to do, and usually they won't make the choice you want them to make.

It was late Saturday morning. Mother and Lizzie had already headed out to do some shopping and go to the movies to see a matinee, so I knew they would be gone for the day. I knew Landon was home alone. Mrs. Whitman and Emily had left early to do some shopping in Columbus and stay overnight. Sure must have been nice to shop the way those two did! Emily skipped school all the time to go shopping.

I decided I would head to the house and see if I could find Landon. I was sure he was still sleeping, sick as he'd been the night before. It was time for us to have a talk even though I knew he wouldn't be very cooperative since he was dope-sick. I knocked on the back door, but no one answered. I waited a few minutes before I went inside. I yelled for Landon several times but didn't get an answer. I searched his room, the bathroom, and the basement. I couldn't find him. I decided I would go out to the garage. If his car was gone, then I'd know he wasn't home.

Wow—how was I going to do this? I was afraid I was going to lose my nerve. Whenever I saw him, part of my anger faded to sadness and I could never seem to say what was really on my mind. I really needed to stand my ground this time. I couldn't live like this and neither could he. He *wouldn't* live like this; he would end up dead. All the books say addicts end up in one of three places if they don't get help: in jail, in an institution, or dead.

I'd prayed so many times that Landon would get caught by the cops. Maybe then his parents would find out and a court would force him into getting help. His parents I could tell, but the cops, never. I couldn't do that to him. I might have prayed for it, but I wouldn't be the one to do it. So that left the other two options, and neither of them was desirable.

I had to confront Landon and let him know that if he didn't tell his parents, I would. Did that make me a snitch? I didn't want to be a snitch, but Landon's life meant more to me than my reputation. Would his mother even believe me? She didn't like me at all. I would never forget the way she'd looked at me the day I'd arrived here, like I was some piece of trash.

The first thing I saw when I walked into the garage was Landon's Mustang, and the second thing I saw was Landon passed out in the driver's seat of the car. I'd heard him pull out of the driveway not long after I'd lain down, but I had no idea what time he'd come back. He was out of control.

My heart felt like it was going to jump out of my chest. I suddenly knew what the expression "blood boiling" meant, because I could feel it. It was like I was a volcano on the verge of erupting. Every part of my body felt like it was on fire. I stormed over to the car and said Landon's name. He didn't budge. I said it a little louder. Nothing. I could feel the tears welling up in my eyes. Oh no! No tears. I would not let them make me look weak. I was sticking to my guns.

I looked around the garage for something to use to bang on the car and I spotted a baseball bat. I went over and got the bat from the corner, but as I was approaching the car, I tripped over an extension cord and landed right behind the Mustang. The bat flew out of my hand and crashed through Landon's rear windshield. Landon came out of that car screaming!

"What the hell are you doing?"

I raised myself off the ground and said, "Trying to wake you up."

"By busting out my windshield? Nice, Jane. Looks like you succeeded. I'm awake now."

He was furious.

"I tripped. I didn't intentionally bust out your windshield. I'm sorry; I'll pay for it."

I shouldn't have said that. I should have let him think I'd done it on purpose. Maybe then he would have understood how upset I was.

"You tripped? Well, how did that bat end up in my backseat then?"

"I grabbed the bat to make some noise," I explained. "I tripped over this freaking extension cord and the bat flew out of my hands. I couldn't get you to wake up."

"What was I supposed to think?" he shot back. "I figured you were pissed because I didn't go in the house after you went in last night. You're always mad at me anymore, Jane."

"I *am* mad, and don't give me some crap excuse that you're tired or sick again," I yelled. "I'm not buying it this time. I know you left again after I went into the house last night. Normal people don't fall asleep in the garage. They can usually make it to their bed. I think you were too wasted to make it in the house, Landon.

What did you do after I left you last night? You were supposed to go in the house. Did you really think I wouldn't hear you pull out of the driveway at five this morning? It must have been a good ride, because evidently you found your fix."

It was time for me to hold back nothing. Time to not worry about making him mad and instead to tell him the straight-up truth, whether it hurt him or not.

"Oh, whatever, Jane, here we go again. Is this going to be another lecture on how I'm killing myself? Let's hear it from the addiction expert. This is really getting old, you know? Didn't I just hear all this last night? Why can't you accept that I have this all under control and there's nothing to worry about? I would think you'd be thanking me after I saved your little butt last night. What the hell were you thinking going there? I'm the one who should be pissed. You should have never been there last night."

Landon was walking closer to me.

I took a few steps closer to him so I was right in his face. This was my life he was messing with, and it was time for me to speak my mind.

"That's crazy stuff you've got yourself into," I told him. "Those people are nuts. I agree: I was a complete idiot for going there. But I was so worried about you. I'm pretty sure that explosion had something to do with a meth lab. How can you associate yourself with that kind of crap, Landon? Who knows what Uncle Mac would have done to me last night."

He stuck his finger right in my face.

"Jane, you don't peek into a dope dealer's windows. You could have been killed. You're lucky there was an explosion, because I don't know if I could have gotten either one of us out otherwise. I'll be surprised if Mac doesn't come looking for us."

I was shaking. Did he really not get it?

"See, that's just it, Landon. You don't understand that I would risk my own life to save yours. I would march right up to an army of drug dealers. Was it stupid? Hell yes, it was stupid, but I would do anything for you."

"You act like I do nothing but mess up all the time," Landon protested. "I think you're just looking for something else to nag at me for. Every time I think I'm getting something right, there you are telling me I've done something else wrong. I can't win with you, Jane. Nothing I do is good enough for you. You want me to be somebody I can't be, and quite frankly I'm getting tired of it."

I smacked his finger out from in front of my face.

"Landon, you make me feel like the biggest bitch in the world. I do feel like I bitch at you all the time. I love you; I don't want anything to happen to you. That's why I'm on you about it all the time. I would like nothing more than to not worry about you. But I do and I won't apologize for that. I won't. I don't want to do this anymore. Not like this."

He backed away from me and threw his arms up in the air.

"Really? Is that what you want? Is that where this is going? You don't want to worry about me anymore? Are you telling me you're done then, Jane? You're done with me?"

I stepped closer to him. I was not going to let him walk away from me. We were going to finish this conversation with nothing left unsaid.

"That's not what I want, Landon. I want you, but not this way. I've been through all of this once before, and my sanity cannot take a second round."

He was starting to calm down a little.

"Jane, it doesn't sound like you're giving me a choice. It sounds like it's going to be your way or no way. Why does it have to be your way?"

"I want this for me, Landon, but I want it more for you. My way will keep you alive. You could hate me for the rest of my life and I wouldn't care as long as I knew you were healthy and safe. I don't want to lose you. It would kill me to know I wouldn't be able to see your face every day, even if that face despised me. I know you think I'm being silly and paranoid about everything, but you need to realize that, at any moment, what you're doing could take your life. Would you want me to live my life carrying the guilt of you losing yours? I would carry that guilt for all my days because I sat back and did nothing but watch you die. Heck, I didn't just watch—I gave you permission. I have a decision to make also. Do I let you kill yourself or do I rat you out to your parents and you hate me forever? So if you don't choose to tell them and get help, then I will. You get to make the decision about our future, but I'm making the decision about yours."

There. I'd put it all out there. I didn't know what he would say. I was so scared. Would he choose to walk toward our future or would he choose to walk out of my life? I couldn't stand to wait for his response. I walked over to the car and leaned against it with my head down. It was quiet for a long time.

I couldn't take it anymore, so I turned around and raised my head to see what he was doing. He was still standing in the same place he had been. He was staring right at me. He walked over to me and stood directly in front of me. He looked down at my face and gave me the meanest look I could have ever imagined. I was scared to death of what he was about to say. He stooped down so his face was right in front of mine.

"Jane, I will not be told what to do. This isn't fair. I don't ask you to change. I love you, but I will not put up with this anymore. I'm done. And so help me, if you say anything to Mom and Dad,

I'll never speak to you again. Do you understand me? Never."

He kissed my forehead and headed toward the door. I fell to the ground before he made it out the door. To this day, I'm still not sure how I made it back to my bedroom. I was shocked. I don't know why, because deep down I'd known that would be his choice.

I stayed in my bedroom for two days. I cried more than I'd ever cried in my life. I'd known this outcome was a good possibility when I'd given Landon his choices, but I'd given them to him anyway. I'd known it would hurt, but I'd never dreamed I would feel like I would never be able to breathe again. It felt like Landon had shot a hole straight through my heart. I kept telling myself this was better than the alternative. I could live through this; I could *not* live through Landon's death.

I didn't go to school Monday. Mother thought I was staying in bed because I was sick. I didn't tell her any different until Monday night after Lizzie had gone to bed. I got up and went into the living room. It was time I talked to Mother about everything. It was the first time in years I'd actually talked to my mother about anything other than what I had to. But I told her everything. I told her about how I felt about her and how I was finally starting to trust her again. I told her about how serious my relationship with Landon was. I told her about Landon's drug use and how it had broken my heart that I couldn't help him. She told me she would help me talk to Mrs. Whitman. It was something I had to do. I knew Landon was going to hate me forever. It hurt to know that, but I had to do it.

I stayed home again Tuesday, but this time it was so Mother and I could go talk to Mrs. Whitman. Mrs. Whitman was nicer than I'd expected. She'd never liked me, but she seemed to have a soft spot for my mother. Mrs. Whitman listened intently as Mother told her everything I'd shared. Mrs. Whitman asked me why I would choose to tell her everything about Landon if I loved him so much. I explained to her that it was *because* I loved him so much that I had to tell her. I just couldn't have handled it if something were to happen to Landon and I hadn't done anything to prevent it. Mrs. Whitman actually apologized to me and told me she'd misjudged me. I couldn't believe it.

She expressed her concern for Landon and grabbed her laptop right away to find a rehab center. Oh my gosh! Landon was really going to hate me now. I sat there in a daze while Mother explained to Mrs. Whitman how rehab worked and how it had changed her life. When we left, Mrs. Whitman was on the phone making arrangements for Landon to enter treatment. She'd decided to buy a drug test and test him when he got home from school. She said if he tested positive, she would take him straight to the rehab center.

Mother asked me if I wanted to go somewhere so I wouldn't be home when Landon got back from school. I didn't want to go anywhere. I wanted to see him before he left. I had to, even if it was only through my window. I didn't want to face him, but I wanted to see him. I hadn't seen him since he'd kissed me goodbye.

I saw him come in from school about 3:45 p.m. It wasn't until about 5:30 that I heard him outside yelling at Mrs. Whitman. She was loading luggage into the back of her car. They got into Mrs. Whitman's car and drove away. I haven't seen Landon since. Watching them drive away was heartbreaking.

I missed school the first couple days Landon was gone. I didn't want to do anything. I didn't want anyone to touch me or even look at me. I didn't want to talk to anyone; I didn't want to see anyone; I just wanted to sit and stare. It was like the world was going on as if nothing had changed. Couldn't anyone see that it *had* changed?

Landon was gone, and even when he came back, he might never speak to me again. I couldn't bear it; I really couldn't. I tried to move, but it felt like my limbs weighed too much for me to move them. They were so heavy. The first night he was gone, I'm pretty sure I had an anxiety attack. My face felt like it was on fire, the rest of my body was freezing, I was shaking, and my feet and hands felt so cold. How could someone feel so miserable, relieved, sad, happy, lonely, scared, and angry all at the same time? I was so glad Landon was somewhere he could get help and get healthy again, but I was so angry that he was gone. The drugs had taken him from me in a whole other way. I should have been thrilled that he was getting help. And I was; I really was. I just missed him so much. I'd thought it was hard to love an addict who was actively using, but I'd never dreamed how hard it would be to have him taken from me. I wanted to go get him and bring him home, but that would have been very selfish of me. I knew I couldn't, because I wanted him to get better. That was all I'd ever dreamed of since I'd found out Landon was on pills. I didn't want anything bad to happen to him. I wanted him to realize he could live life without the drugs.

I was scared that if he did decide to forgive me, he might realize he didn't really love me. Evidently, he'd been high the entire time I'd known him. When he started to live life sober, would he even like me? I probably shouldn't have worried about it, because I was sure he wasn't going to forgive me for what I'd done.

Landon was in my dreams every night. They were crazy dreams, but some way or another he was always in them. I missed him so much. I needed to see him, smell him, and touch him. I just needed him.

I missed several more days of school and avoided all phone calls. I pretty much just stayed in bed and tried to sleep the time away. I think I'd been in bed about nine days when I woke up to Milah Jo yelling at me to put my damn boots on and to pull my big-girl panties up. She stayed there all day bugging the crap out of me until I agreed to go to school the next day. I knew she was right; staying in bed wasn't going to make things any better. I couldn't believe she still cared about me after the way I'd treated her the past few months. Between obsessing over Landon and losing my mind once he left, I hadn't even talked to Milah Jo much.

● ● ● ● ●

The next month of school was really rough without Landon. I don't know how I could have gotten through it if not for Milah Jo, Luke, and Mother. Luke was a senior; he'd started sitting with me and Milah Jo at lunch. I'd noticed him around before, but he was a loner like I was and had never really said much. He'd been really helpful. He'd decided I could use a friend since pretty much everybody at school hated me and thought I was a narc. Both of Luke's parents were addicts. He lived with his aunt and uncle because his parents were in prison for trafficking. He was really easy to talk to because he got it. He understood what it was like to love people who love drugs. He got why I did what I did and didn't give me a hard time about it like almost everybody else in this stupid farm school.

Kyle made sure to let everyone at school know I'd ratted Landon out to his parents. Emily had finally left me alone. I guess that was her way of agreeing with me. But I had new hate graffiti to deal with. It had become a daily thing to see "Narc" or "Rat" on my locker. I didn't think Emily was behind it, though. Apparently I had new haters.

I'd really considered doing the home-school thing on the internet. I'd gotten pretty used to being a loner, so losing the social aspects of my high school years didn't sound all that bad to me. Mother wouldn't hear of it, though. She said I had to stick it out. She also had this theory that if those kids couldn't see that I'd done the right thing, then they weren't worth my time anyway. Mother just kept telling me that doing the right thing was never easy and that things would get better. She said that one day Landon would thank me for what I'd done. I didn't believe that, though. I just knew he would hate me forever.

Mrs. Whitman had been keeping us updated on Landon's progress. She kept telling us he was doing really well. She showed us a picture of her visit one weekend and Landon looked great. Mrs. Whitman said he'd gained twenty-two pounds since he'd been in treatment. He did look really good. She said he really liked the AA/NA part of his treatment.

Landon was sixty-three days into a ninety-day program when I got a letter from him. I was shaking when I opened it. I had no idea what it would say. It took me a whole day before I finally got the courage to open it.

Dear Jane,
I'm not sure of what to say. I'm at a loss for words. I believe the last thing I said to you was that I would never speak to you again. I was wrong. I am so sorry. I don't think I could go through my life with never speaking to

you again. I have been angry at you for a long time. I couldn't understand why you would do this to me. You said you loved me and yet you told Mom everything and she sent me here. Through the help of my counselor, I have realized that you did it because you loved me. I put you through so many things you should have never gone through. You had already been through so much with your mother. I didn't realize how bad I had gotten until my head was clear and I could see all that I had done.

I am working the steps of AA/NA. I am on step nine. It tells me I need to make amends with everyone I hurt. I know I hurt you. You mean the world to me and I treated you the worst. I understand now that you were trying to help me. I am so sorry. I hope one day you can forgive me. I get to come home in twenty-seven days; I hope you will give me a second chance. I understand if that isn't possible. I do hope, however, that we can remain friends because I do want you to be a part of my life. I love you so much, Jane. Please don't give up on me yet.

Landon

• • • • •

I couldn't believe he really wanted to try to work things out. He had said he would never speak to me again and I'd been sure he would hate me forever. I'd finally started to come to grips with knowing he would never be a part of my life again. Now, after reading this letter, the thought of him coming home and wanting me sent shock waves right through my stomach. It was all I'd dreamed about.

I wasn't sure what it would be like when Landon came home. Would he truly forgive me? Would I be able to trust him again? I'd gotten so paranoid toward the end, I'd practically tracked every move he'd made. I couldn't do that after he came home. For him to be able to get better, I would need to be able to give him back some trust. I couldn't be questioning his every move. I wasn't sure how to do that because I knew I would always wonder if he was out getting high. I didn't know if I could truly hand over my heart again that easily. It had happened so accidentally the first time. I'd never meant for it to happen.

The problem was he already had my heart. He would always have my heart. He hadn't given it back to me the day he'd left. In fact, I think he might have taken it with him. That made it an easy decision for me to make: I had to give him a second chance. There was no other choice for me. I loved him so much.

I'd learned a lot lately. I'd come to believe that everyone should get a second chance and that some things take hold of us whether we want them to or not. The drugs took hold of Landon, and Landon took hold of me. We never start out thinking we'll lose control of ourselves, but before we know it, something else is controlling every part of us.

I would give Landon that second chance. I would count down the days until he came home. Yes, *home*. This was home now. This small town in this little county had become my home, and I loved every bit of it thanks to Landon showing me how beautiful it was.

Acknowledgments

A special thank you to my family for putting up with all my book craziness and encouraging me to get it done. A huge thank you to my family and friends for supporting me and helping me share this story with the world. Your support is everything.

To my Papa, may you rest in heaven. The pride you showed every time you told someone about this book filled me with so much love. You always treated me as if I were going to do great things, and I will forever miss you.

To my mom, you were always the best mother a child could have ever wanted and now you are gone. You will never know how you are so very missed. I will forever be grateful for everything you always did for me. You were my rock and my safe haven. What will I ever do without you?

And to my daughter, everything I do is for you, kiddo. I love you to the moon and back. You have grown into an amazing young woman, and I couldn't be prouder of you. Always go after your dreams; you can do anything you want.

About the author

Jessica K. Baker drew upon her personal experiences with loved ones battling addiction as she wrote her first book, *Opiate Jane*. Jessica also spent five years working in the addiction field as a counseling assistant and a social work assistant. Jessica, who has a degree in human and social services, shares her life in Ohio with her teen-aged daughter, Annie.

Printed in the United States
By Bookmasters